BIRD OF PREY

"Do you know a man named Clint Adams?"

"Of course I know him," Dillon said, trying to act unimpressed. "They call him the Gunsmith."

"He's in Alton."

"And?"

"And I want you to get him out of Alton."

"That's all?"

"That's all. Oh, one other thing."

"Yeah?"

"How you do it is your business," Lawrence said. "I just want you to do it by the end of the week."

"This is gonna cost you."

"I'll pay you whatever you want," Lawrence said. "Just do it."

Dillon stood up. "Consider it done."

THE GUNSMITH

206

LEGEND OF THE PIASA BIRD

J. R. ROBERTS

JOVE BOOKS, NEW YORK

LEGEND OF THE PIASA BIRD

A Jove Book / published by arrangement with
the author

PRINTING HISTORY
Jove edition / March 1999

The Penguin Putnam Inc. World Wide Web site address is
http://www.penguinputnam.com

ISBN: 0-515-12469-9

A JOVE BOOK®
Jove Books are published by The Berkley Publishing Group,
a member of Penguin Putnam Inc.,
375 Hudson Street, New York, New York 10014.
JOVE and the "J" design
are trademarks belonging to Jove Publications, Inc.

PRINTED IN THE UNITED STATES OF AMERICA

10 9 8 7 6 5 4 3 2 1

PROLOGUE

As he rode along the Mississippi, the great river was taking all of Clint Adams's attention until he looked up and saw the huge bird on the bluffs above him. At least, he thought it was a bird. It appeared to have horns like a deer; red eyes; a beard like a lion on the face of a man; a body covered by green, red, and black scales; and a tail so long it went around the body, through the head, and between the legs.

If it had been real it would have been monstrous and frightening, but as it appeared to be painted on the side of the bluff it was simply breathtaking. Clint had no idea that something like this could actually be painted on the side of a bluff. He also had no idea why anyone would do such a thing.

The last thing he noticed was that the bird appeared to have arrows clutched in its talons. Clint wondered, then, if this was the work of some local tribe of Indians, and if this was their god.

He found himself staring at the bizarre painting for a very long time before shaking his head and then looking around as if embarrassed. Of course, no one else was around, but he still felt as if he'd been caught doing something he shouldn't have been.

1

He got Duke moving once again, continuing to ride along the Mississippi, but there was nothing on the river at the moment, or over on the Missouri side, that could rival the spectacle on the bluff. He found himself looking over his shoulder again and again until finally he seemed to round a bend and the "bird" was out of sight. He kept on going, fighting the urge to turn around and go back for another look.

ONE

The first town he came to after seeing the painting on the bluff was called Elsah. It was a small place right on the Mississippi and for this reason Clint decided to stop there. He also figured that someone there might know something about that bird he saw painted on the side of the bluff.

He left Duke at the livery, which was on one of Elsah's two main streets, got himself a hotel room, and then went to one of Elsah's two saloons. If anyone would know anything, it would be a bartender.

Clint ordered a beer and asked his question.

"Sure, I know what it is," the bartender said. "Everybody here does."

"Well, I'm not from here," Clint said, "and I don't mind telling you it scared me half to death."

"That's the Piasa bird," the man said.

"The what?"

"Piasa," the man said slowly, pronouncing it "pie-a-saw." "Piasa bird."

"What does Piasa mean?"

Now the man frowned. "You know, that I don't know," he said finally. "I only know what the thing is called."

"Well, who can tell me what it actually is?"

3

"Is it important?"

"Well, no, it isn't important," Clint said. "I'm just curious."

"Well, now," the man said, rubbing his blue-jowled face, "and this is just a guess, mind you, but I'd say ask an Indian."

"An Indian?"

"Yeah."

"What Indian?"

"Any Indian," the bartender said. "Any Illini Indian, I guess."

"Are there any in town?"

The bartender rubbed his bristly jaw again, then looked down the bar. "Hey, Leon. Is old Charlie an Illini Indian?"

Leon, standing at the bar with a half-finished beer, looked at the bartender and said, "Yeah, I think so."

"And where do I find old Charlie?" Clint asked.

"Around," Leon said.

"It's a small town, mister," the bartender said. "Around ain't that hard to find."

"Thanks."

Clint spent the day trying to find the Indian called old Charlie, wondering why he was bothering. Every so often he'd ask someone about the Piasa bird, but no one seemed to know more than how to pronounce the word and that the painting was there.

He went to the other saloon in town and encountered more of the same. It was later now and girls were working the floor of the saloon. They all smiled at him and swished their skirts at him, but one in particular caught his eye. She had dark hair and darker skin than the others. Most saloon girls he knew made a point of staying out of the sun. They wanted to keep their skin pale. This one had an outdoors look to her. Beneath her skirts, her calves seemed to have a muscular look to them, and there was no loose skin anywhere on her arms or shoulders. Her breasts were full and firm. She was not slender and certainly not heavy. The only word he could think of to describe her was . . . healthy.

"You don't want her," someone said to him.

He turned to find one of the girls, a rather skinny blonde, standing next to him.

"What?"

"I see you're looking at Amanda."

"Is that her name?"

"You don't want to bother with her."

"Why not?"

"She's not your type."

"And what's my type?"

"Me," she said, putting her hand on his arm. "I'm much softer and sweetersmelling than she is."

"Is that a fact?"

"Women are supposed to be soft, don't you think?"

"Not all the time."

"What?" She pulled her hand away.

"In fact," he said, "I think you're wrong about me. I happen to like strongly built women."

"Strongly built?" she repeated, blinking. "And what am I?"

"Well," he said, "for my taste, ma'am, you're just a little bit . . . skinny."

"Skinny?" She put her hands on her hips and her eyes flashed angrily. "Who are you calling skinny?"

"Maybe," he said then, "we should just forget about it, ma'am."

"And don't call me ma'am," she said. "My name is Ellie."

"All right, Ellie," he said. "It was nice to meet you, but I guess I'm just not interested. Okay?"

"Hmph!" she said, and flounced off.

Clint picked up his beer and turned his attention back to the woman he now knew was called Amanda. He enjoyed watching her move around the room, and he knew that she knew he was watching.

"Hey."

A man's voice this time. He turned and saw that the fellow was tall, over six feet, and beefy, though by no means fat.

"Whataya mean callin' Ellie skinny?" the man demanded.

Clint just stared at the man and thought, Shit.

TWO

"I asked you why you called Ellie skinny," the man demanded again.

"Look, friend," Clint said, "there's been some mistake."

"Yeah," the man said, "yours. See, me and the boys, we don't think she's skinny."

Clint had to lean back to see that there were two more men behind this big one—the "boys" he was talking about. Also behind him was Ellie, looking very smug at the moment—and, truth be told, a little on the skinny side.

"What I said to the lady was meant as a compliment," Clint said, trying again to appease the man before trouble started.

"Well, she didn't take it as no compliment," the man said. "You gotta apologize to her."

Clint leaned back again so he could see Ellie and said, "I'm sorry, Ellie. I didn't mean to say you were skinny."

The man turned and looked at Ellie, to see if she was satisfied.

"That's it?" she asked him. "That's all you're gonna do after he insulted me?"

"He said he's sorry," the man said.

"Nate," Ellie said, folding her arms across her small breasts, "I thought you said you loved me."

"I do—"

"And that you'd do anything for me."

"I would—"

"Then you got to show this man he can't go around insultin' the woman you love." She leaned toward the man. "You gotta hurt him."

Nate turned to face Clint with a look on his face so apologetic he looked like he might cry.

"I gotta hurt you."

Well, that got the attention of everyone in the saloon. Apparently Nate hurting someone was a local attraction.

"Now, wait a minute—"

"I'm sorry, mister," Nate said again, flexing his huge hands.

"Nate, you and the boys—"

"The boys won't do nothin', mister," Nate said, "just me."

"No, no," Clint said, "you won't."

Nate frowned.

"Why not?" He looked puzzled.

"Because, Nate," Clint said, "I'll shoot you before I let you hurt me."

The puzzled frown deepened.

"But I ain't got a gun."

"I don't care."

"You'd shoot me and I ain't got a gun?"

"That's right."

Now he really looked like he was going to cry.

"That ain't right."

"Well, hurting somebody just because Ellie tells you to isn't right, either."

"But," Nate said, as if it made perfect sense, "I love her."

"Well, I'm glad you love her, Nate," Clint said, "but

did you ever think that maybe she doesn't love you?''

Nate turned and looked at Ellie.

"Of course I love you, Nate," she said. "He's just tryin' to confuse you. Go ahead, he won't shoot you."

"Mister," Nate said, "I gotta."

"So do I, Nate," Clint said, putting his hand on his gun. "If you make a move to hurt me, I'll shoot you. I promise."

Nate stared at Clint for a while longer, then said, "Aw . . ."

As he started to move, suddenly someone darted between Nate and Clint. It took him a moment, but he recognized it was Amanda.

"Nate, you big lug, stop it!" she snapped. She pressed both of her hands against his chest.

"My Ellie wants me to hurt him, Amanda."

"He'll shoot you, Nate," she said, "and Ellie won't care."

"She won't?"

"Of course I will," Ellie said, glaring at Amanda, "but he won't shoot, Nate. You're unarmed."

"Nate," Clint said, "I'm wondering why a woman who says she loves you wants to get you shot so bad."

Clint looked past Nate at his two friends. He noticed that neither of them was armed, either.

"If you fellas are his friends, you'll get him out of here."

"Nate," one of them said, "Amanda's right. This fella will shoot you."

"Come on, Nate," the other man said. He gave Ellie a look and added, "She ain't worth dyin' for."

Nate turned, reached out, and grabbed the front of the man's shirt.

"That's my Ellie you're talkin' about, Burt."

"Nate," the other man said, grabbing his wrist, "let him go. Come on, cut it out!"

Reluctantly, Nate let the man's shirt go.

"Come on, Nate," the first man said, "let's get out of here."

He finally got Nate moving toward the door.

"We're sorry, mister," Burt said.

"That's okay."

When the three men were outside the saloon, Clint's hand relaxed.

"Why'd you have to stick your nose where it don't belong?" Ellie snapped at Amanda.

"You were gonna get Nate shot, Ellie."

"He said I'm skinny!"

"Well," Amanda said, "you are. I'm always tellin' you that."

Ellie looked Amanda up and down and said with contempt, "I don't see how he can want you instead of me."

She turned and stalked away, and everyone lost interest and went back to what they were doing—or what they were drinking.

"Is that right?" Amanda asked, turning to face Clint. "What she said?"

Clint noticed how much prettier she was up close.

"That's what started the whole thing, I guess. Maybe I shouldn't have told her that."

"Maybe you and me should have a talk."

"If you like—"

"Later," she added, cutting him off, "after work."

"That'd be fine," he said. "Do you know anything about the Piasa bird?"

She smiled and touched his arm.

"I know about lots of things, mister," she said. "Just meet me here about three."

"I'll be here."

As she walked away Clint watched her swish her hips.

"Hey," the bartender said from behind him.

"Yeah?"

"Would you really have shot Nate?"

Clint looked at the man. "If he was going to hurt me? You bet."

"But . . . he was unarmed."

"He had his hands," Clint said, "and they looked pretty deadly to me."

THREE

Clint was still standing at the bar, nursing the second beer, when the sheriff of Elsah entered.

"Uh-oh," the bartender said.

"What?"

The man inclined his head and Clint looked at the man with the badge. He was a stocky man of middle years, clean shaven, his clothing so cleanlooking he might have only recently dressed—except it was after midnight.

"Another boyfriend of Ellie's?" Clint asked, on a hunch.

"You bet."

The man came over to the bar where Clint was standing. He gave Clint a short look, then switched his gaze to the bartender.

"Understand we had a little trouble in here earlier, Pete."

"Who told you that, Sheriff?"

"Never mind," the sheriff said. He looked at Clint again. "This the fella?"

"What fella is that, Sheriff?" Clint asked.

The lawman turned to face him head-on. He was a few inches shorter than Clint, but didn't look intimidated by it. Clint noticed that the man smelled of some kind of soap, as if he'd just bathed.

"I understand you threatened to shoot one of our citizens," the sheriff said. "An unarmed citizen."

"A seven foot unarmed citizen."

"What?"

"Are we talking about Nate . . . somebody?"

"Tremayne," the sheriff said, "Nate Tremayne. He's big, but he ain't seven feet."

"Okay," Clint said, "six and a half, whatever. I still wasn't about to let him get his hands on me."

"So you threatened to shoot him?"

"Damn right."

"And would you have?"

"Damn right," Clint said again.

"Mister," the lawman said, "you're lookin' for trouble."

"I was just having a beer, Sheriff," Clint said. "I didn't start anything."

"I understood you bad-mouthed one of the girls here."

"I don't think so," Clint said.

The sheriff looked at Pete, the bartender.

"You know Ellie, Sheriff," he said. "If a man don't fall at her feet, she thinks she's been bad-mouthed."

"That ain't the way to talk about Ellie, Pete," the sheriff said.

"Hey, look," Clint said, "how many boyfriends does this skinny blonde have?"

"Now, wait a minute—" the sheriff started, pointing a stubby forefinger at Clint.

"What's your name, Sheriff?" Clint asked, cutting him off.

"What?"

"Your name?"

"It's Blaine, Sheriff Rick Blaine."

"Well, Sheriff Blaine," Clint said, "I just don't happen to be interested in your little Ellie. She decided to try to get me beat up. When that didn't work I guess she sent you in to scare me. That's not working, either. Why don't we just forget the whole thing now and let me have a pleasant visit to your little town.''

The sheriff seemed flustered, fought to regain his composure, but he knew that he did not have the upper hand here. That confused him. After all, he was the one wearing the badge.

"Look here . . ." he said, then paused, then started again. "How long do you plan on staying in Elsah?"

"Until I find something out."

"What's that?"

"I'm interested in the Piasa bird."

"The . . . what?"

"The bird painted on the side of the bluff," Pete said. "You know, the Piasa bird."

"Oh, that," Blaine said.

"Do you know anything about it?" Clint asked.

"I don't know nothin' about a bird," Blaine said. "What's your name, mister?"

"Clint Adams."

The sheriff's reaction made it obvious he knew the name. Clint also felt the bartender stiffen behind him.

"Adams?" the sheriff asked.

"That's right."

The sheriff took two steps back and licked his lips. He looked across the room, and Clint followed his eyes and saw Ellie standing against a wall, her arms folded.

"Is she the queen bee of this town?" he asked either Blaine or Pete.

"She thinks so," Pete said.

"Sheriff?" Clint asked. "You want anything else?"

"Uh, no," Blaine said, "no, I, uh, I'm just doin' my job, you know."

"If that's all you were doing," Clint said, "I wouldn't mind, but you're letting some blond gal—some skinny

blond gal, at that—make you and your badge look silly—
don't you think?''

"Uh, maybe you're right . . .''

"Now, I'm not looking for trouble, but I'm not going to
let anyone run over me, either. I don't care who it is. I'll
be in town a couple of days at the most, and I'd like to
avoid trouble. That good enough for you?''

"Uh, sure,'' Blaine said, "good enough for me.''

"Well, then,'' Clint said, pointing across the room,
"make sure she knows that, too, okay?''

"Uh, sure,'' Blaine said, "I'll tell her.''

"You do that,'' Clint said, turning to face the bar and
his beer. "I think we're done here.''

The sheriff didn't know what to say to that so he backed
away some more, then turned and walked from the saloon.
Clint noticed that Ellie went out after him, but that was the
lawman's problem.

FOUR

"So, you're the Gunsmith, huh?" Pete asked.

Clint didn't answer.

"Guess ol' Nate is lucky he didn't have a gun, huh?"

Again, no answer.

"You want me to get you a colder beer?" the man asked. "That one must've got warm."

Clint pushed away the half empty beer and said, "Sure, why not?"

Pete cleared the bar and hurriedly placed a fresh beer in front of him.

"Look," Clint said, "I don't want my name getting all over town."

"Sure."

"I mean, I know how bartenders like to talk."

"I get ya," Pete said. "Not a word from me."

"I'd like to think you're telling me the truth," Clint said, "but somehow I doubt it."

"I ain't a liar, Mr. Adams," Pete said, putting his hand over his heart.

"I'm not saying you're lying," Clint said. "You just might not be able to help yourself."

Pete's eyes narrowed. "You been talkin' to somebody about me?"

"No," Clint said, "I just think all bartenders suffer from the same disease."

"What disease is that?"

"Big mouth."

Clint was waiting outside the saloon when Amanda came out.

"What was that about?" she asked.

"What?"

"The sheriff?"

"Can't you guess?"

Her eyes widened. "That stupid bitch Ellie tried to send him after you, too?"

"She did send him after me," Clint said. "I had to talk him out of doing something silly."

"Shall we go to your hotel," she asked, "and talk there?"

"Maybe we can talk along the way, too," he said, extending his arm so she could slide hers through.

"About what?" she asked as they started walking.

"The Piasa bird."

"Oh, that."

"You did say you knew something about it, didn't you?" he asked.

"Well . . . I know there's a painting," she said, "and I know it's big . . ."

"You don't know who painted it?"

"No."

"Or when?"

"No."

"Or what it actually is?"

"I'm sorry," she said, "no."

They walked on to the hotel in silence until they had almost reached it.

"I'm sorry," she said again, "when you said you wanted to talk I thought . . ."

"It's okay," he said, "we don't have to really talk."

"Well . . . good."

They went through the lobby, the desk clerk studiously avoiding looking at them. They went up the stairs, down the hall, and stopped in front of his room.

"You should know something," he said, before unlocking it.

"What?"

"I don't pay for . . . well, talking."

"Mister," she said, "I could feel your eyes on me from across the room. I'm not looking for money tonight."

"Oh," he said and unlocked his door.

FIVE

She had the firmest breasts he had ever encountered. In fact, her entire body was firm, not an ounce of fat anywhere but without sacrificing her feminity.

He stood looking at her, wondering who would make the first move. He didn't have to wonder long because before he had barely closed the door she backed up against him, pushing him tight against the wall.

Rubbing her firm ass against his dick, she grabbed his hands and squeezed them to her chest. "Hurt me, pinch my nipples."

He did as she said.

When she could feel him getting hard, she reached behind her with one hand and undid the front of his pants. "You like that, don't you?" she asked.

"Having a beautiful woman touching me like that, why wouldn't I like it?"

Leaning forward she then pulled her skirt up and lowered her underpants, squirming out of them until they were on the floor, draped around her ankles. Removing one of his large hands from her breasts, she moaned and put it between her legs. "Make me wet. I want to be so wet you can slide right inside and make me happy."

"I think that would make us both happy," Clint said, working his fingers deep inside her.

But his erection was making his legs weak, and the more she squirmed and moaned the more he pushed against her smooth, firm buttocks until he couldn't stand it anymore.

Dragging her across the room to the bed, he tore at her dress, ripping the fabric, desperate to get to her. When she was completely naked, he stripped his own clothes off and climbed on top of her.

She grabbed for his dick like she was holding on for her very life, squeezing it so tight he would have objected if it didn't feel so good. She was the kind of woman who liked to be in charge, Clint could see, and he was the kind of man who would let her—this time.

Spreading her legs wide, she shoved him into her wetness then clamped her legs around his waist. "Come on, Clint, show me what you're made of."

He pounded into her, driving his desire into her. Her skin was hot down there. He buried his face into her neck, licking and kissing a trail from ear to ear. All he could think about was tasting her skin, licking her sweat, digesting every inch of her.

Her hair was matted along her forehead as their perspiration fell onto the sheets. She stared him straight in the eyes. "You got the finest ass I've ever seen." She raked her nails across his backside, making him jerk forward.

Then she moved like she was going to start wrestling him. Before he knew what was happening, she had him on his back and was straddling his glistening body. "I can make you go deeper inside this way," she said. While she pumped him, she leaned back and massaged his balls with her hands. The sensation drove him to loud grunting.

When Clint was almost ready to come, she climbed off him and knelt between his legs. "This is gonna be the best you ever had," she said, checking his eyes. Then she took him into her mouth and sucked. . . .

• • •

Later they changed positions. He settled down between her legs and used his mouth and tongue on her, trying to make it the best she had ever had. When he had erupted into her mouth, he had to admit that if it wasn't the best it had certainly been in the top five. Now he wanted to leave her with the same impression.

She was strong. Her stomach was flat, and as he rested his arms on her he could feel the muscles in her thighs. When he slid his hands beneath her to cup her ass and lift her up, he marveled again at how firm her cheeks were, especially when she was clenching them, as she was now.

"Jesus," she said, straining beneath him, "you're gonna kill me. . . ."

No, he thought, not kill, just impress . . . and then she was bucking and writhing beneath him, as he did just that.

SIX

Later Clint and Amanda lay side by side together with the sheet on them. She asked him if he wanted her to leave and he said no. She could stay or go as she pleased.

"Why are you so interested in that bird?" she asked.

"It's unusual," Clint said. "I've never seen anything like it. I'm curious."

"Mmmm," she said.

"Have you seen it?"

"Oh, yes," she said, "I've seen it many times."

"Didn't you ever wonder who painted it?"

She thought a moment, then said, "No, I guess I haven't."

"You're not curious at all?"

"No."

Clint shook his head, wondering how anyone could take such a thing for granted.

"How long have you lived here?"

"All my life."

"And how long has it been there?"

She shrugged and said, "As long as I can remember."

That would explain it, then. If she'd seen it since she was a little girl it was old news to her.

"Your parents never talked about it?"

"No."

"You and your friends?"

"No," she said. "Why would we? To us it's just always been there."

"Well, it's new to me," he said, "and I'd like to find out more about it."

"Who else have you asked?"

"Everyone I've seen," he said. "Nobody seems to know anything about it. Pete told me about an Indian named Charlie. Do you know him?"

"Oh, sure," she said, "everyone knows Charlie."

"Do you know where I can find him?"

"No," she said. "I don't know where he lives. He's just always around."

"Well, I'll have to start looking for him tomorrow," Clint said. "That is, if your friend Ellie doesn't send some other boyfriends after me."

"She's not my friend."

"Why does she have so many men after her and you don't?"

"I don't know," she said. "I guess most men just like blondes."

"Skinny blondes," he said. "What I like about you is that you're not skinny."

"Is that so?"

"I mean—that's not to say—I didn't mean to imply that you were, uh—"

"Never mind," she said, saving him. "I know what you mean, and I appreciate it."

"How long have you worked in the saloon?"

"A few months," she said. "Only since the school closed."

"The school?"

She nodded. "I was the schoolteacher, but the town ran

out of money for it and had to close it. Working in the saloon was all I could find.''

''Why not go someplace else where they need a teacher?'' he asked.

''This is my home,'' she said. ''They claim they'll be able to reopen it soon. I want to be here when they do.''

''And the town doesn't mind you working in the saloon?'' he asked. ''They'll let you go back to teaching their children?''

''They say they will,'' she said. ''They better not be lyin' to me. Hey, I just serve drinks, I'm not a prostitute.''

''I'm sorry, I didn't mean—''

''Stop apologizing so much,'' she said, cutting him off. ''You're not offending me. In fact,'' she added, sliding her hand down his leg, ''anything but.''

When she touched his cock it almost leaped into her hand.

''Mmm,'' she said, fondling it, ''ready again already?''

''Ready,'' he said, rolling toward her, ''willing, and able . . . teacher.''

SEVEN

In the morning Amanda woke early, woke him and strad-
dled him, taking him inside of her even before he was fully
awake. By the time she was finished with him, though, he
was both awake and newly exhausted.

"I have to go," she whispered to him.

He watched sleepily—but with pleasure—while she got
dressed, and then she leaned over him and kissed him ten-
derly.

"Have fun finding your bird," she said to him and
slipped out the door.

He fell right back to sleep.

He awoke just an hour later, feeling refreshed and hungry.
Briefly, while he dressed, he wondered where a schoolteacher had learned all of the things they had done together
during the night if—as she claimed—she was not a prostitute. He certainly knew that all women who worked in
saloons were not "professional" girls—but a great many
of them were. Still, he had no reason not to take her at her
word.

He finished dressing and went downstairs for breakfast.
The hotel had a dining room, although it was a small one.

29

Lucky for him no one else was there and he got extra good service.

After breakfast he left the hotel with the intention of finding the Indian called old Charlie. Unfortunately, he didn't know the first place to look.

He took a turn around town and didn't see anyone who even resembled an Indian. When that was done he decided to saddle Duke and take a ride out to take a better and longer look at the Piasa bird painting.

He found it with no trouble. It seemed to him that the odd bird was proudly looking down at the Mississippi. When he got closer he could see that it had a rather fierce countenance, and he doubted very much that this bird was considered a benevolent god by the Indians—if, indeed, it was one of their gods.

He dismounted and sat on a rock, staring up at the painting. He marveled at himself and his fascination for the painting. He wanted to know everything about it: the legend of the bird and who had painted it. Also, who had discovered the painting.

The face of the bluff was sheer. For someone to paint it they would have had to be lowered down from above. He knew that Chinese workers were lowered over cliffs in baskets to plant charges when the railroads were extending west and needed to blast through the rock cliffs. He wondered if this painting had been achieved in the same manner.

Suddenly, while he was staring at the painting, he thought he saw something above it. He frowned. It had been a movement out of the corner of his eyes. He looked up at the top of the bluff now, to see if anyone was there. He watched and waited, and just as he was about to move his eyes he saw it again. It was colorful, whatever it was, a large, and . . . could this be? It seemed to have wings.

This wasn't possible. Surely this Piasa bird was a painting, and a legend, but it couldn't really exist . . . could it?

He decided to find his way to the top of that bluff and see what he could find.

It took him some time to find a path to the top of the bluff, and one that was big enough for Duke to negotiate. Finally, he found it and made his way to the top. He dismounted and walked to the edge of the bluff. Looking down he could just make out the color on the wall of the bluff, but he could not make out the shape. Still, it was enough to tell him that it was, indeed, the painting of the Piasa bird that was below him.

He turned and walked back to where he had left Duke. He studied the ground, but there was no indication that anyone had been there. Still, he had seen *something*, he knew that for sure. He was not the sort of man who hallucinated for no reason.

Perhaps he was still in bed and had been so exhausted by a night with Amanda that this was all a dream. He closed his eyes, then opened them again, determining that he was not dreaming. This was real, and he may have seen something that *looked* like the Piasa bird.

Looked like, because it certainly could not have *been* the creature whose likeness graced the bluff wall.

That would be impossible.

He rode Duke back down the path, studying it for recent usage. Suddenly, he saw something and reined the big gelding in. He dismounted and started to walk toward what he had seen, but lost sight of it. Then he saw it again, a flash of red or orange, and it was moving.

He stopped in his tracks. It was floating in the air, blown about by the breeze, and he could see it very clearly now as it actually began to blow toward him.

It was a big orange and red feather.

EIGHT

Clint rode back to town with the big orange and red feather in his saddlebag. He still wasn't ready to admit that he had seen a real Piasa bird, so he wasn't going to mention the feather to anyone. He still wanted to find Charlie, though, and decided to go to the sheriff to see if he could help. Maybe the man was intimidated enough to be of assistance.

He reined in Duke right in front of the sheriff's office and looped the reins carelessly over the hitching post. Duke wasn't going anywhere, anyway. The big gelding instinctively knew when his job was to run and when it was to just stand still.

Clint opened the door to the office and stepped inside. The sheriff was in the act of pouring himself a cup of coffee and Clint's appearance arrested the movement for a moment.

"What can I do for you, Mr. Adams?" Sheriff Blaine asked. He finished pouring his coffee and carried the cup to his desk. He didn't offer Clint a cup.

"I'm looking for somebody, Sheriff."

"And who might that be?"

"An Indian people hereabouts call old Charlie."

Blaine looked surprised.

"What do you want with Charlie?"

"I just want to ask him some questions."

"About that bird painting?"

"That's right."

"What's got you so interested in that?"

Clint felt exasperated. Was he the last person in the world with an ounce of curiosity?

"I'm not from around here, Sheriff," he said. "I'm not used to seeing something like that. I'd just like to find out more about it, that's all."

"Well," Blaine said, "I can't help you. Charlie comes and goes as he pleases."

"Is there anybody in town who might know? Somebody he talks to?"

Blaine rubbed his chin for a few moments, set his coffee cup down on the desk, and sat back in his chair. He looked like a man who was trying to appear relaxed.

"You might talk to Will Gentry."

"Who's that?"

"You met him when you put your horse in the livery," Blaine said. "He owns the stables and sometimes Charlie does some work for him."

"Okay," Clint said. "That's all I wanted to know. Thanks for your help, Sheriff."

"Sure thing," Blaine said. "Enjoy the rest of your stay."

Now he was the magnanimous host.

Clint left the lawman's office and rode back to the livery. He had, indeed, met Gentry briefly when he handed Duke over to him. Like most men who had worked with horses all their lives, Gentry's hands showed it. There were countless scars from nips and bites over the years, and he remembered that the man had a vicious-looking scar on his cheek.

Gentry looked up from his work as Clint walked Duke

into the livery. He was a well-fed-looking man in his sixties with strong if somewhat gnarled hands.

"Mr. Gentry," Clint said, "can I talk to you for a minute?"

"Somethin' wrong with yer animal?" the man asked.

"No, he's fine," Clint said.

"He's a good-looking beast, that one. Can't say as I ever seen a sturdier-lookin' animal in all my years around horses."

"Thanks," Clint said. "We've been together a long time, Duke and me."

"Good animal's hard to find, these days," Gentry said. He wiped his hands off on a rag and tossed it aside. "What kin I do fer ya, then?"

"I'm looking for an Indian called old Charlie," Clint said. "I understand he works for you sometimes?"

"When he's a mind to," Gentry said. "Ol' Charlie's a right good hand with horses. Been at it almost as long as I have. Don't know how he done it, but he's got almost no scars to speak of. Reckon Injun ponies don't bite as much as white man's horses. See this one?" He pointed to the scar on his face. It took up most of his right cheek, starting just below the eye.

"Bad one," Clint said.

"You said it," Gentry said. "Likely bled to death after that animal took a bite out of my face."

"Lucky you didn't lose an eye."

"You got that right," the older man said. "Happened thirty years ago, and I've learned a lot since then."

Like how to keep your face away from a horse's mouth, Clint thought.

"Can you help me?"

"With what?" Gentry asked. "Oh, Charlie."

"Do you know where he lives?"

"Nope," Gentry said. "Nobody does. What do you want with him, anyway?"

"I want to ask him some questions about the Piasa bird."

"That bird painted on the bluff?"

Clint felt relieved. At least someone knew what he was talking about without his having to explain it first.

"That's right. Do you know anything about it?"

"Might of, once."

"What do you mean, once?"

"Well, I forgit things, lately," Gentry said. "Comes from bein' eighty-three, I reckon."

"What?" Clint was shocked. The man didn't look a day over sixty-five.

"Don't think anybody should live this long," Gentry said, more to himself than to Clint. "Forget more'n you remember."

The man seemed pretty sharp to Clint.

"Well, if you see Charlie, would you tell him I'm looking for him? I'll pay him to talk to me."

"You let that be known around town and that might draw him out," Gentry said.

"I'll do that."

"Want me to take care of your hoss?"

"Sure, thanks," Clint said, handing over the reins.

"One other thing might get Charlie to talk to you."

"What's that?" Clint asked. "Good whiskey?"

"This here animal," Gentry said. "Nothin' ol' Charlie likes better'n good hossflesh."

"You don't mean . . ."

Gentry cackled, catching Clint's meaning.

"No, I don't mean to et!" he said, still laughing. "He just appreciates it. He'll have a lot of respect for a man who owns a hoss like this one."

"I don't own him," Clint said. "We just travel together."

"That was the right thing to say, mister," Gentry said. "Yep, I think you and ol' Charlie are gonna get along jest fine."

Sure, Clint thought, if I ever find him.

NINE

When Clint left the livery he had the feeling that Will Gentry was a lot sharper than he liked to let on. He also had the feeling that old Charlie would soon hear that he not only wanted to talk to him, but that he would pay for the privilege.

For want of something better to do, Clint went back to his hotel room. He found that he was tired, probably from the strenuous night he'd spent with Amanda. Maybe he was getting too old for . . . nah, that couldn't be it. Whatever the reason, he removed his boots, hung his gun belt on the bedpost, and was soon deeply asleep.

Something woke him. He didn't know what, but he'd heard something. He sat up in bed and looked around the room. He spotted the piece of paper someone had slipped under the door. Had that been the sound that had awakened him? Or had whoever delivered the note been a little noisy in the hall?

He walked over and picked up the note. One line was scrawled in an almost unintelligible hand: "If you want to know about the bird on the bluff go to Alton."

Clint had seen a road sign for Alton. It was further south

along the Mississippi, between Elsah and St. Louis. He didn't know why he hadn't thought of it himself. If the people in the small village of Elsah knew nothing about the Piasa bird, why not ask the people of a larger place, like Alton?

What he didn't understand about the note was whether or not it was suggesting that if he went to Alton someone would meet him there. Or was it simply a suggestion? Whatever it was, it was a good idea, and he decided to act on it immediately.

He checked out of the hotel, fetched Duke from the livery, and went to Alton.

TEN

While Elsah was a small village that had been bypassed by major steamboat traffic because of low water levels, as well as the railroad and major industries, Alton was so successful that it had incorporated as a city in 1837. It said so on a sign just outside the city limits. THE CITY OF ALTON, INCORPORATED 1837.

High on the bluffs that overlooked the city were huge, palatial mansions. The port was busy, as was the railroad station. Its streets were not only wide but extremely attractive, and as he rode in he could see that there was an overabundance of businesses. During the ride to the livery stable he also saw more churches than he'd ever seen in a town or city before. He was also going to have his pick of hotels.

The liveryman here was younger than Gentry in Elsah—much younger. Obviously, he was too young to own the business himself, so he was an employee. Clint quickly sized the young man up and decided he'd unsaddle and rub down Duke himself before finding a hotel.

When that was done and the big gelding had been fed, Clint carried his saddlebags away from the livery, along with his rifle, and stopped at a hotel called the Stratford. It was a huge hotel that was on a hill, which was why it caught his eye. After staying at that little hotel in Elsah, he decided to treat himself to something better. The only thing he'd ever seen to rival this was in a big city like San Francisco or New York, or the time he was on Mackinac Island, in Michigan.

He got into his room and looked out the window and found he was looking down on the city of Alton. He could see the docks, littered with arriving and departing steamboats, and the busy streets, filled with people going about their day's business.

Upon leaving Elsah he had told two people where he was going. First, he'd made sure he said good-bye to Amanda, who expressed surprise that he was leaving already.

"No one in Elsah can seem to help me," he'd told her. "It makes sense to go to a larger city. Maybe the information I want will be there."

"Will you be back this way?"

"It's possible," he'd told her, but he'd made no promise.

Second, he told Will Gentry, so that if he did hear from old Charlie, he could tell the Indian where he was.

He got settled into his room and wondered what to do next. He decided that two places were likely to have the information he wanted. One was a local newspaper, and another was the local library. As an incorporated city, Alton was bound to have a free library that was supported by taxes.

He left his room to check on both of those.

The newspaper office was a bust.

"We don't go back far enough for that," the editor said when Clint asked about stories about the Piasa bird. "Try the library."

"Good idea," Clint said, and asked for directions.

• • •

The librarian Clint spoke to was named Emma Jean Lawrence, a young woman in her twenties who wore no makeup but was very pretty nonetheless.

"The Piasa bird," she said. "Yes, I believe we have some material on that."

"Really? That's great."

"Come this way," she said, leading him down a hall. "Have you seen the painting on the bluff?"

"Yes, I have," Clint said. "That's what got me interested."

"It's beautiful, isn't it?"

"Very," he said. "I went to Elsah to see if anyone knew anything about it, but they don't."

"It's amazing," she said, "how people can take such a thing for granted."

"Exactly what I was thinking."

"I'm happy to see a man such as yourself interested in it."

"Such as . . . what kind of man is that, Miss Lawrence?" he asked.

"Oh," she said, stopping and turning to face him. "I've offended you. I'm sorry. I just meant . . ."

"What?"

"A . . . Western man," she said. "I mean . . . with, with your gun and your clothes . . . you must admit you don't look like the type of man who would be interested in art."

"You'd be surprised, Miss Lawrence," he said, looking her right in the eyes, "the things I find interesting."

She seemed flustered for a moment, then said, "Uh, yes, well, this way, please."

She took him to a large sitting room with wall-to-wall shelves. He was afraid she was going to leave him there alone. The time he'd spent in libraries could be counted in seconds rather than minutes and hours. He would have been lost and that would have confirmed her opinions about "Western men."

"I'll get you the books," she said, and he breathed a sigh of relief behind her back. All he needed now, however, was for her to ask him if he knew how to read.

She returned with two books. One was called *Native Americans*, and one was called *Legends*.

"Then the Piasa bird is a legend," he said, looking at the second book.

"Oh, yes," she said. "Is there anything else I can do for you?"

"Not at the moment, Miss Lawrence," he said. "You've been very helpful."

She left him alone, and he opened the book on Native Americans first. The section on the Piasa bird told of Ouataga, Chief of the Illini Indians, who had gathered his people together and supplied them with poison arrows with which to destroy the Piasa bird. There was not much beyond that.

The second book, on legends, described the Piasa bird in more detail, saying that in addition to everything Clint had seen in the painting—the colors, the beard, eyes, the face like a man, and the tail, not to mention the scales—that the Piasa bird was as big as a calf. It also said that it fed on humans.

There was another entry that said the Piasa bird might also be called "the Thunderbird."

There was nothing in either book about the painting.

Clint left the books on the table and found his way back to the main room, where he also found Miss Lawrence.

"Were those books helpful?" she asked.

"A little," he said. "I left them on the table, by the way. I, uh, didn't see where you got them from."

"That's fine, Mr. Adams. Is there anything else I can help you with?"

"Well," he said, "there was nothing in the books about the painting."

"Oh, well . . . perhaps we have some books on art. I could . . . look it up for you and let you know?"

"That would be very helpful."

"Where are you staying? I'll let you know when I find something."

"The Stratford."

Her eyes widened. "That's supposed to be a beautiful hotel."

"It is," he said. "I'll tell you what. If you find something for me, I'll take you to dinner there."

She blushed and said, "Well, I—"

"Just my way of saying thank you for all your help."

"Well," she said, "all right."

"Good," he said, "then I'll wait to hear from you. By the way, my name is Clint. Shall I call you Emma Jean, Emma, or stay with Miss Lawrence?"

She smiled, blushed again, and said, "Emma would be fine."

As he left he had the feeling she would be, too.

ELEVEN

Clint was surprised that twenty-five miles north of St. Louis—a city he'd been to many times—there was a city like Alton, which he had never heard of. It seemed to be a city proud of its history. For one thing it was the site of the Lincoln-Douglas debates in 1858, on Broadway and Market Streets. There was also a Confederate graveyard. It was the home of Illinois's first state penitentiary, built in the 1830's, which had been used as a military prison for Confederate soldiers—over 1300 of whom died during a smallpox epidemic.

Alton was also a stop of the famed Civil War Underground Railway.

Clint learned these things by talking to the hotel desk clerk, and then walking around the city. He was also advised to look at the city's Christian Hill and Middletown districts, which was where many of the mansions and estates were. Some of these were built by the industrialists who came to town to set up their businesses, and many of them were designed by Lucas Pfieffenberger, a local architect who was also mayor of Alton. Other homes were built by German immigrants who first settled in Alton during the 1840's and 1850's.

Alton was also the home of Lyman Trumbull, who lived there from 1855 until his death in 1873. He was the author of the Thirteenth Amendment of the Constitution, which abolished slavery.

Clint walked around Alton, thinking to make himself visible. He still didn't know if the author of the note meant to contact him there.

Before having dinner he checked back at his hotel to see if there were any messages from Miss Lawrence. There was one, saying that she had found out some information for him, and would be at the library until six o'clock. He returned to the library at 5:45.

Clint insisted on keeping his promise of dinner at the Stratford. Emma Jean Lawrence protested that she was not properly dressed, but Clint assured her that she would probably be the loveliest diner in the hotel dining room. She blushed prettily, and they headed for the hotel.

She marveled at the lobby, and then even more at the dining room.

"This place is as beautiful as I've heard," she said, as they were seated.

The waiter discussed the menu with them in detail and then took both of their orders for dinner—salmon for Miss Lawrence and a steak for Clint.

"I'm afraid I don't have much imagination when it comes to food," he said to her.

She was afraid he was again referring to what she had said that afternoon about "Western Men" and started to apologize again.

"No, no," he said, "I'm serious. I've been to some of the finest restaurants in New York, San Francisco, even London, but I'm still a confirmed meat and potatoes man, I'm afraid."

"You've traveled quite extensively, then," she said, obviously impressed.

"Yes, I have," he said. "Being unmarried allows me that luxury."

"You've never been married?"

"No," he said. "It wouldn't be fair to any woman. I know how much I like to travel."

"Where else have you been?"

They talked for a while about South America and Australia. He found himself pleased that he was breaking the mental picture of the Western man that she had formed over the years. Over dessert, though, he started to feel silly that he was trying so hard to impress this young woman.

"So tell me," he said, "what did you find out about the Piasa bird painting?"

"Oh, yes," she said, reaching for her purse. "I took some notes."

He waited while she retrieved them.

"The painting was first discovered in 1673 by Father Jacques Marquette, when he came down the Mississippi with Louis Joliet."

He waited, but it quickly became apparent that she was finished.

"But who painted it?"

"I . . . don't know."

"So it's just been there for at least two hundred and ten years and nobody knows who painted it?"

She looked disappointed. "No," she said. "I couldn't find anything on who the artist was. I'm sorry."

He reached across the table and touched her hand.

"Hey, that's okay," he said. "You've been real helpful, Emma."

"I suppose I could keep looking," she said.

He smiled and said, "If I thought I needed an excuse to see you again I would agree."

"You . . . want to see me again?"

"Well, I need someone to show me around Alton," he said. "How about it?"

"Well . . . all right," she said. "I'll have to take some time off from the library, but . . ."

"I'll bet you could use some fresh air," he said. "Are there some good spots for picnics?"

"I don't know."

"Well, where did you go the last time you were on a picnic?"

She looked down. "I've never been on a picnic."

"What's wrong with the men in this town?" he asked. "No one has ever taken you on a picnic?"

She shook her head.

"I find that hard to believe, Emma."

"My work at the library keeps me very busy," she said. "And I do other volunteer work . . . and then there's my family."

"Your family? You mean, like, a husband and children?" he asked.

She blushed and said, "Oh, no, I'm not married, and I certainly don't have any children. I mean, I want children someday, but . . . no, I meant my father and my mother. And I have a brother and a sister."

"Oh, that kind of family."

"Do you have any family?"

"None that I know of," he said. "I came west from the east years ago, but . . . I don't know of anyone."

"Don't you ever get lonely?"

"I have a lot of friends," he said. "Bat Masterson, Wyatt Earp . . ." He spoke without thinking.

Her eyes widened. "You know those men?"

"Well, yes, we're friends."

"They're notorious! We have books in the library about them."

"They're just men," he said, "and they're my friends."

She was looking at him funny then, and he thought he knew what she was thinking. Maybe she didn't recognize his name, but he had a feeling she was going to go to the library tomorrow and look through those books on notorious men to see if she could find him.

There had been plenty of dime novels written about him. He wondered if any of them were in the library, and if they were, he wondered what she'd think of them.

TWELVE

Clint offered to show Emma his room, but she blushed and declined.

"I would like to show *you* something, though," she countered.

"And what's that?"

"My home," she said. "Would you come there for dinner tomorrow night?"

"I'd be delighted," he said.

She wrote the address on a slip of paper and handed it to him.

"Just give this to a cab driver. He will know where to take you."

"I'll look forward to it," he said, putting the address in his shirt pocket. "Can I take you outside and get you a cab?"

"Thank you."

They walked outside together, and Clint had the Stratford doorman fetch a cab for Emma. He then walked her to it and helped her inside.

"Until tomorrow night, then," she said.

He took her hand and kissed it, causing her to blush more furiously than before.

"Until tomorrow night," he said, and the cab drove away.

Clint turned to go back inside the hotel, but then decided to take a stroll. The night air coming off the Mississippi was fresh and damp, and he enjoyed the way the cool air felt. Maybe, somewhere along the way, he'd find a likely looking saloon and go in for a drink.

"A cab, sir?" the doorman asked.

"No, thank you," he said. "I'm a guest, but I'm going to walk a bit."

"As you wish, sir."

"Where might I find a saloon or two that would supply an evening's diversion?" Clint asked.

The doorman laid a finger alongside his nose and asked, "An evening's diversions, sir . . . or a night's?"

Clint smiled, taking the man's meaning perfectly.

"No, no," he said, "just an evening."

"You might try along Broadway, sir," the doorman said. "Plenty of places there."

"Thank you."

Clint tipped the doorman for fetching the cab and for the information, then started walking in the direction the man had indicated.

THIRTEEN

Broadway was indeed filled with saloons, and there was noise coming out of all of them. Clint kept walking, looking for a place where he could get a drink without having to put up with the racket. Finally he found one, a small place with no voices or music coming from inside. He had to turn off of Broadway to find it, though, and found himself on the corner of Front Street. Front Street extended down past the docks, and the saloons and taverns along there offered a somewhat different quality of entertainment than the establishments along Broadway. Since this one was right at the very beginning of Front Street, though, and barely half a block from Broadway, it was sort of a combination of the two types of saloon.

As he entered he saw that the place was well filled without being crowded. There was a table or two to be had, and plenty of room at the bar. However, his appearance seemed to be of interest to all present, and they watched him as he walked to the bar.

"Beer, please."

The bartender stared at him a moment and then drew him the beer.

"Thanks," Clint said. "Nice place."

"Yes, sir. Thank you."

Clint lifted the mug to his lips and had a few swallows of cold beer. By the time he set it down there was a man standing on either side of him.

"Lost your way, have you?" one of them asked.

Clint looked at him, and then at the other man. Both were wearing clothes that led him to believe they were employed aboard one of the steamboats docked nearby.

"I don't think so," he said. "I just came in for a beer, and here it is."

"Is it good?" the first man asked.

"Yes, it is."

"And cold?" the second man asked.

"Yep."

"We don't usually get strangers in here," the first man said.

"I see," Clint said. "It's a regular hangout, then?"

"You could say that," the second man said. "Whenever we're in Alton, it's where we drink."

"When we can afford the price of a beer," the first man said.

Clint saw where this was going and decided to head it off.

"Well, then," he said, "let me buy you fellas a cold beer."

"Well," the first man said, "that's right neighborly of you, friend."

The first man turned to the other patrons in the place and said, "This stranger says he's buyin' drinks for the house."

Clint couldn't get a denial out fast enough and so was being pummeled on the back by all of his new friends as the bartender hurriedly served beers all around. By that time it was, of course, too late.

Clint spent the evening buying drinks for the regulars at this particular tavern, who sang his praises more loudly the drunker they got. Finally, he had to leave because the place simply became too noisy, the very reason he'd passed up so many other places earlier that evening.

He made his way back to his hotel and up to his room. He was in the process of removing his boots when he fell asleep. Consequently, he spent the night with one boot on and one boot off.

When he woke the next morning he couldn't remember exactly where he had been drinking the night before.

FOURTEEN

Clint spent the next day in futile pursuit of someone who knew something of the Piasa bird painting. Apparently, Alton being further from the bluff than Elsah, the people of the city were even less informed of its origin.

He did, however, see more of the city of Alton during the day, and even made his way down to the docks to see if he knew anyone aboard any of the steamboats. He thought, perhaps, he might find his friend J. P. Moses— who owned a gambling boat—there, but he did not. It was just as well, for if he had he would have had to put it down to coincidence, and he sorely hated coincidences.

On his way back to his hotel he did not pass the saloon in which he had drunk the night before. That, too, was just as well, for he didn't relish being once again buffaloed into buying drinks for the house.

When he got back to the hotel he indulged in a long, hot bath before dressing for his dinner at the home of Emma Jean Lawrence. He knew, from the sheer number of blushes he saw on her lovely face the day before, that he would not be dining alone with her. It was more than likely he would be meeting the entire Lawrence family that evening. Perhaps one of them would know something of the Piasa bird painting, even if she did not.

• • •

That evening Clint stepped from the Stratford Hotel, wearing a suit of clothes he had purchased earlier in the day. He gave the doorman the address where he was going and asked him to fetch him a cab.

"Will the driver know where that is?" he asked.

The doorman looked at the address, then at Clint in surprise.

"Why, yes, sir, I believe any cab driver would be familiar with this address."

"And why is that?"

"Because, sir, it's in the Middletown District."

"I don't under—"

"It's one of our wealthier districts in Alton, sir," the man said.

"I see."

The doorman left him to get a cab, and Clint wondered what he had stepped into. He hadn't expected a young lady working in a library to be part of one of the wealthier families in town. She certainly hadn't told him that she was, but then she hadn't told him that she wasn't, either.

"Your cab, sir," the doorman said.

Clint gave him a tip he hoped wasn't too small, considering where he was going for dinner, and got into the cab.

"Do you know where we're going?" he asked the driver.

"Oh, yes, sir," the man said, "I know it well."

"Let's get going, then," Clint said and sat back in the cab.

The homes that they passed along the way were at first modest, then larger, and then considerably larger and more expensive. The closer they got to their destination, the more impressed Clint became with the family of Emma Jean Lawrence. He remembered how she had said she did a lot of volunteer work. He assumed, then, that the library was one of the places she volunteered. He was almost certain that no young lady who came from a family that lived in this district would have to actually work for a living.

When the cab came to a stop, the driver leaned down and said, "We're here, sir."

When Clint stepped down from the cab he found himself facing perhaps the largest, most elegant-looking house he'd ever seen, bar none in Boston, New York, or London.

"Are you sure we're in the right place?"

"Yes, sir. This is the address I was given."

Perhaps Emma's father *owned* the library in which she volunteered.

"All right," Clint said and paid the man. "Thank you."

"Thank you, sir," the cab driver said. "It's not often I get to drive into this part of the city. Wait until I tell my wife."

"And I hope she enjoys the story," Clint said.

He turned and looked at the house once again. It dwarfed any multi-columned house he'd ever seen on any plantation in the South. He prided himself on his ability to remain unimpressed in the face of wealth, and up until now he had been successful at it. Perhaps it was just the surprise of finding such a house in the city of Alton—which was, after all, *not* St. Louis—that was adding to his surprise.

He took a deep breath and proceeded up the walk to the front door.

FIFTEEN

Emma must have been waiting for him, because the large oak door opened before he could reach it, and she stood in the doorway. She was wearing a high-necked dress that covered her from head to toe, and she looked lovely. The dress hugged her figure to the waist, where it flared and reached to the floor. Her lower half matched her upper half; she was indeed lovely from that head to those toes.

"Clint," she said, reaching for him with both hands.

He mounted the steps and took her hands.

"Hello, Emma. This is an incredible house."

"Are you angry with me?"

"About what?"

"Well . . . I didn't tell you that my family had money."

"It wouldn't have made a difference in my accepting your dinner invitation."

"Well," she said again, "you weren't entirely truthful with me, either, were you?"

"About what?"

"About who you are."

"Emma," a man's voice said, "have you lost your manners, leaving our guest on the doorstep that way?"

"I'm sorry, Poppa," she said, and then pulled on Clint's

61

hands. "Come in and meet my father," she said.

Clint entered and found himself in a huge entry hall. Above him a huge chandelier gleamed. A man in his sixties, heartily built, his hair snow-white, approached him with his hand out.

"Wendell Lawrence, sir," he said, shaking Clint's hand. "You are the Clint Adams my daughter has talked so much about since returning home last night?"

"I suppose I am," Clint said, unaware of what Emma must have told her family about him.

"Well," Lawrence said, "in truth she's talked of you more this evening than last."

Emma looked down at the floor and said, "I looked you up when I went to the library today."

"I see."

"If half of what she's told us is true," the older man said, "we're in for an interesting evening."

"Poppa!" she said, scolding her father shamelessly. "You promised."

"Now, now, Emma," Lawrence said, "I won't force the man to tell us any stories he doesn't want to tell us."

Little did Wendell Lawrence know that Clint didn't want to tell *any* stories.

This was not going to be a good night.

He was wrong.

Emma's mother was a charming, handsome woman in her fifties, who managed to keep her husband in check for the entire meal. Luckily, Emma's brother and sister were not at dinner. There was no explanation about where they were, and he didn't expect one.

Wendell Lawrence did start a few sentences with, "Emma tells us you're some sort of gunman," and, "We understand you're some sort of Western legend," but each time her mother, Ellen, cut him off.

Clint found out that Emma's family didn't own the library, and that she really was a salaried employee there, "though not much of a salary," her father was quick to add.

"Our Emma says she feels like she has to make her own way in the world," he went on.

"I think that's admirable," Clint said.

"So do I," Ellen Lawrence said, "but her father thinks it's silly."

"Why should she have to work when she's from the wealthiest family in Alton?"

Not "one of" the wealthiest families, Clint noticed, but "the" wealthiest family. Of course, Wendell Lawrence did qualify that with "in Alton." Clint wondered where the man would rank if he took in the whole of Illinois.

Dinner was served by two servants, a woman and a man, both of whom were white.

"Since this was a stop on the Underground Railroad during the war," Wendell said at one juncture, "it wouldn't do to have black servants, would it?"

Clint just nodded. He still wasn't quite sure what to make of Wendell Lawrence. They had not discussed where the family money had come from. He wondered if Lawrence had inherited it, or if he was a businessman who had made his own fortune. At the moment he did not seem to have the kind of brains it took to be a businessman. He also seemed to have no tact—but that never held anybody back in business, that Clint knew of. In fact, most of the wealthy men he'd known over the years had little or no tact.

They had dessert and then Wendell Lawrence stood up and said to Clint, "Join me in the study for a cigar, Mr. Adams."

"Thank you, Mr. Lawrence," Clint said after a moment. As he stood up to follow the man, he saw Emma mouth to him the words, "I'm sorry." He didn't know if she was apologizing for something that had already happened or what was going to happen.

He followed Wendell Lawrence across the huge entry hall and down another hallway to the study.

SIXTEEN

Lawrence gave Clint a cigar, lit it for him, then gave him a snifter of good brandy. Then he got one of each for himself. After that they each sat in an expensive, overstuffed easy chair, facing each other.

"I want you to know," Lawrence said, "that I am not impressed by your reputation."

"Well, that's good—"

"I'm fascinated by it, I admit," Lawrence went on, "but not impressed."

"I don't like talking about my reputation, Mr. Lawrence," Clint said.

"And why is that, sir?"

"Because I usually end up trying to defend it."

"Is it indefensible?"

Clint hesitated. He'd never thought of his reputation in quite that way, but now . . .

"Maybe it is."

"Is it true?" Lawrence asked.

"What's your reputation, Mr. Lawrence?"

"You're answering a question with a question, sir," the other man said. "Some men would see that as being somewhat evasive."

"Believe me, Mr. Lawrence," Clint said, "I'm answering your question."

"Very well," Lawrence said, "I have a reputation—I think—as being a hard businessman."

"And a smart one?"

Lawrence hesitated, then said, "No, I can't say that's part of my reputation."

"How do you feel about that?"

"I don't like it."

"Why not?"

"Because I think I am a smart businessman."

"Well," Clint said, "that's how I feel about my reputation."

"That doesn't quite answer the question," Lawrence said. "May I continue?"

"Please do."

"Emma says there are many books on you in the library—dime novels, she calls them—describing you as a gunman. Do you see yourself as a gunman, Mr. Adams?"

"I see myself as a man who is good with guns, Mr. Lawrence."

"Using them? Or building and repairing them?"

"Both."

Lawrence drew deeply on his cigar and allowed the smoke to trickle from his nose.

"Then the name that you carry, 'the Gunsmith,' is not just a name?"

"No," Clint said. "I am a qualified gunsmith."

"Do you ply this trade?"

"I did, once," Clint said. "I traveled about with a wagon and equipment."

"And what happened?"

"Men wouldn't let me be a gunsmith," Clint said. "They were too busy forcing me to prove that I was *the* Gunsmith. Do you understand what I mean?"

"I believe I do, sir," Lawrence said. "I believe I do."

They sat in silence for a while, and then Lawrence broke it.

"I see your point now in asking me about my reputation," he said. "I hope you will forgive my behavior to this point."

"I'm a guest in your home," Clint said. "It's not for me to criticize or judge your behavior."

"You're kind."

More silence, again broken by Wendell Lawrence.

"And now, sir, I must ask you what your intentions are toward my daughter."

Clint closed his eyes for a moment and drew on his cigar as a diversion. This was going to be the part that wasn't any fun.

SEVENTEEN

"My intentions?"

"Isn't that what fathers are supposed to ask?" Lawrence asked.

"Of suitors, I suppose," Clint said, "or potential suitors."

"And you are neither?"

"Mr. Lawrence," Clint said, "I just arrived in town yesterday, went to the library, and met your daughter."

"But . . . you had dinner together."

"She helped me out, and I asked her to dinner as a thank you."

"And then she invited you here?"

"I suppose to repay me for the dinner last night."

Lawrence frowned. "Well . . . you are a little old for her."

Clint didn't know what to say to that.

"What brought you to Alton, sir?"

"The Piasa bird."

"I beg your pardon?"

Was it possible that Wendell Lawrence didn't even know about the painting?

"The painting on the bluff of the Piasa bird?" Clint said.

Lawrence's puzzled frown deepened.

"I'm afraid I haven't the slightest idea of what you're talking about," he said finally. "Why don't we rejoin the ladies?"

He didn't have to ask Clint twice. Lawrence rose and walked to the door, leaving behind his half-finished brandy and his cigar smoking in the ashtray. Clint did the same and followed him. He supposed that's what having servants was all about.

"How did the inquisition go?" Emma asked, pulling him aside when she could.

"It was fine," Clint said. "He was just . . . curious."

"About what?"

"Me, you . . . me mostly, I guess."

"We have to talk about you," she said. "Later."

He didn't know exactly what she meant, but at that moment they were pulled back into the sphere of her parents. Maybe her father thought he was too old for Emma, but her mother seemed to already be grooming him to join the family.

"I'm sorry Emma's brother and sister weren't here," she said as Clint was getting ready to leave. "You'll have to come back and meet them."

"I'd like that," Clint said.

"Edward and Melissa will be thrilled."

"I'll walk you out," Emma said and pulled Clint away from her mother.

Outside she said, "I'm so embarrassed."

"Why?" he asked. "You must have known they'd be like that when you brought a man around. Haven't they done it before?"

She looked away and blushed.

"You're the first man I've ever invited here," she said.

"What? You've never had a young man to dinner?"

"No."

"Well, no wonder they reacted that way," Clint said. "Now I understand better. There's no need to apologize or be embarrassed—but now you'll know what to expect the next time you have a man over."

"I suppose."

A cab pulled up in front of the house at that point. It wasn't a public cab, but a private buggy.

"Father arranged to have you taken back to your hotel," she said.

"Well, thank him for me," Clint said. "I won't have to go wandering around this wealthy neighborhood searching for a cab, appearing like some suspicious man looking for a house to rob."

She strolled down the walk with him to the cab.

"I'll keep trying to find something for you at the library . . . about the Piasa bird."

"All right."

"Will you . . . come by?"

"Of course."

They stood there awkwardly for a moment, Clint aware that her parents might be watching from a window. Finally, he took both of her hands in his and kissed them.

"I'll talk to you soon, Emma. Thank you for inviting me."

"Thank you for coming."

He climbed into the back of the fancy coach.

"I'm staying at—"

"I know where you're staying, sir," the driver said. "I'll have you there shortly. Just sit back and relax."

He did so and looked out the window at Emma, who was apparently waiting for the coach to leave before going back inside. She waved, and as the coach pulled away she turned to walk back in, but did so slowly. He had the impression that she would rather have been going a lot of other places than back into her father's house.

EIGHTEEN

When Clint got back to his hotel it was early. He thought about going out to try to find the tavern where he'd been the night before but decided against it. It had been a good enough place to drink once, but it had ended up being pretty damned expensive. Instead he nodded at the doorman and started inside.

"Sir?" the man said.

"Yes?"

"You are Clint Adams, aren't you, sir?"

"That's right."

Clint took his closest look at the doorman since his arrival at the Stratford. It was the same man who had gotten him a cab for Emma, and then given him directions to Broadway the night before. He was a tall, wide-shouldered man in his forties, wearing some sort of semimilitary-looking uniform.

"Sir, there are some men inside waiting for you to come back."

"Men?"

"Yes, sir," the doorman said. "Two of them. They're waiting in the lobby."

"What's your name?"

"Rocky, sir."

"Do you know who these men are, Rocky?"

"Yes, sir," Rocky said, looking nervous. "Police."

"Alton police?"

"Yes, sir."

Clint frowned. "I haven't done anything in Alton to warrant the police looking for me—that I know of."

Could it be he'd done something the night before while drinking in that waterfront tavern?

"Do you know what they want?" Clint asked.

"No, sir, just that they were asking for you. They called you . . . the Gunsmith."

Clint's frown deepened.

"Is that true, sir?" the man asked. "Are you the Gunsmith?"

"I'm afraid so, Rocky," Clint said. "Maybe that's the only reason they're looking for me. They heard I was in Alton."

"I don't think so, sir."

"Why not?"

"I know these two particular gentlemen," Rocky said. "They're detectives."

"Detectives?" Clint asked. "Not sheriff's deputies?"

"Oh, no, sir," Rocky said. "We have a proper police force here. They're detectives."

Clint paused to think. What could two detectives want to see him about, and was there any reason for him to avoid them? But how could he do that? They knew where he was staying, and by now knew where he was keeping his horse.

"Rocky, thanks for the information," he said, handing the man a couple of dollars.

"Are you still going in, sir?"

"Yes, I'm still going in," Clint said. "I've got nothing to hide that I know of, and I'd like to find out what this is all about."

"Okay," the doorman said, tucking away Clint's money, "you're the boss."

Clint nodded and entered the hotel lobby.

NINETEEN

"Mr. Adams?"

Clint turned to face the two men.

"Clint Adams?"

"That's right."

"Sir," one of them said, "I'm Detective Garrett, this is Detective Stevens. We'd like to ask you a few questions."

"About what?"

Garrett was a tall man in his thirties; his partner Stevens was smaller and a little older. They exchanged a glance and both looked back at him.

"Maybe we can talk about this someplace other than the lobby?" Garrett asked.

"Like police headquarters?"

Garrett smiled. Stevens did not.

"Your room would be good enough, sir."

"All right," Clint said, fishing his key out of his pocket, "let's go to my room."

"Very nice," Garrett said as they entered the room. "I've never been in one of the Stratford's rooms before."

"Feel free to look around," Clint said.

Garrett smiled again. Stevens didn't.

"Why don't we just get down to business," Garrett suggested.

There were enough chairs in the room for them all to sit, but Detective Stevens chose to remain standing. Clint wondered if this was just in case he made a break for the door.

"What's this about, Detective?" he asked, directing the question to Garrett.

"Sir, you were recently in Elsah."

"That's right."

"And you met a saloon girl named Ellie Harold?"

"I don't think—wait, a skinny blonde? That's right, her name was Ellie. I never did know—why? What's happened? Has something happened to her?"

"Why would you think that, sir?" Garrett asked.

"Because," Clint said patiently, "you're asking me about her, Detective Garrett. Why would you be doing that if she was fine?"

"Well, sir," Garrett said, "she's not fine. In fact, she's far from fine."

Clint waited.

"She's dead."

"I'm sorry to hear that. Why come to me? I'm here and she's in Elsah—I presume."

"You got here yesterday," Garrett said. "She was killed while you were still in Elsah, but found later."

"Still, what does it have to do with me?"

Garrett looked up at his partner, who apparently conveyed some sort of message that Clint didn't catch.

"Does he ever talk?" Clint asked.

"Hardly ever," Garrett said. "Sir, we understand you had an . . . altercation with this . . . saloon girl a few nights ago."

"It wasn't an altercation."

"No? What would you call it?"

"I called her skinny," Clint said. "She took offense."

"And then what happened?"

"She unleashed a few boyfriends at me," Clint said. "One big man who intended to hurt me, and then the local sheriff, whatever his name was."

"Blaine," Garrett said, "Rick Blaine. He sent us a telegraph message about you."

"And?"

"Wanted us to question you."

"And you have. Is there anything else I can do for you?"

"We're not quite through, sir," Garrett said. "May I see your hands?"

"Why?"

"The girl was beaten to death."

Clint held his hands out. It was then he saw some broken skin on the left one. When had that happened? And why hadn't he noticed it before?

"Where did that happen, sir?"

"Must have happened in this tavern where I was drinking last night."

"And where was that, sir?"

Clint thought furiously but couldn't dredge up the location of the place.

"I . . . can't remember."

"Convenient," Stevens said. It was the first word he'd spoken.

"The doorman gave me some directions to find a place to drink," Clint said. "On Broadway."

"So this place you went to was on Broadway?"

"It might have been."

"And was there a fight?"

"I don't know," Clint said.

"Do you have any other injuries?" Garrett asked. "Bruises?"

"Not that I know of."

"It's odd that a man who makes his way with a gun would allow his hand to be damaged that way and not remember it," Garrett said.

"It's my left hand."

"Oh, yes," Garrett said. "And your gun hand is your right one."

"Yes."

"Be damn stupid of you to beat someone to death with your right one, wouldn't it?"

"I wouldn't beat someone to death, Detective," Clint said. "It's not my style."

"Oh, that's right," Garrett said, "you'd shoot them."

"I'd shoot a man if he was a threat to me," Clint said. "I wouldn't shoot a woman or beat her to death."

"Is that so?"

"What reason would I have had to beat this Ellie to death?"

Garrett shrugged. "Maybe you didn't want her sending any more boyfriends after you."

"I don't think so."

"Why are you in Alton, Mr. Adams?"

"I came here looking for some answers."

"About what?"

"The Piasa bird."

"The what?"

"The painting on the bluff," Stevens said then. "Supposed to have something to do with the Illini Indians. Nobody knows who painted it, though. It was found about two hundred and ten years ago."

"Is that a fact?"

"You're the first person I've met who knew that," Clint said to Stevens.

"My partner reads," Garrett said. "He's a scholar. Me, I'm just a policeman." Garrett stood up. "Mr. Adams, we're going to have to ask you not to leave Alton for a while."

"I wasn't intending to," Clint said. "As a matter of fact, I've made a friend here."

"Really?" Garrett asked. "Who would that be?"

"Wendell Lawrence."

Both detectives stared at him.

"The Middletown Wendell Lawrence?" Stevens asked.

"That's right."

"You're friends with him?" Garrett said.

"Him," Clint said, "and his daughter. In fact, I had dinner there this evening."

The two men exchanged a glance.

"We can check this out, you know," Garrett said.

"I wish you would, Detective Garrett," Clint said. "I can give you the address, if you like."

"We know where to find Mr. Lawrence if we need to talk to him, Mr. Adams," Garrett said.

"Well, good."

They started for the door, and Garrett turned to face Clint again before leaving.

"Remember. Don't leave Alton."

"Not until I find out what I want to know about the Piasa bird."

Garrett shook his head and left.

TWENTY

Clint entertained the idea of going back to Elsah, but that was a bad idea for two reasons. First, the detectives had told him not to leave Alton. Second, there were bound to be some of Ellie's boyfriends who also thought that he had killed her—that is, except for the one who did.

Clint knew he didn't kill her, so it must have been one of the others. The only two he knew of were the sheriff and that fella Nate. Nate was certainly big enough to have beaten her to death, even by accident. He didn't think that Sheriff Blaine had it in him to beat anyone to death—especially not a woman.

But finding out who killed Ellie was not his job. So he decided to just keep doing what he'd been doing, trying to find out about the Piasa bird painting.

The next afternoon he got the hotel kitchen to put together a picnic basket for him, and he took it over to the library with him. Emma was surprised when he walked in, but pleasantly so.

"I'm glad to see you," she said. "I didn't think I would."

"Why not?"

"I thought my parents had scared you away," she said. "Especially my father."

"Well," Clint said, "he did ask me what my intentions were."

She hid her face and then peeked out between her fingers. "He didn't."

"He did."

"I'm sorry," she said, dropping her hands from her face.

"Nothing to be sorry for," he said. "He's just being a father."

"What did you tell him?"

"That we were just friends."

"And what did he say?"

"That I was too old for you, anyway."

"Oh, God . . ."

"Don't apologize again," he said, holding up one hand. "What's in the basket?"

"Food," he said, "and wine. You do like wine, don't you?"

"I love wine."

"And food?"

"What kind of food?"

"Cold chicken."

"I love cold chicken."

"Can you get away for a picnic?"

"Now?"

He nodded. "Right now."

She bit her lip.

"Come on," he said, "just this once use the fact that you're Wendell Lawrence's daughter. Get the rest of the day off."

"Okay," she said, "give me a minute."

"I'll wait outside."

He went out in front of the library to wait. While he was there a young man came bounding up the steps, then stopped when he saw Clint.

"Can I help you?" Clint asked as the young man stared at him.

"Are you Clint Adams?"

Clint quickly assessed the situation and found that the young man was unarmed.

"I'm Edward," he said, "Edward Lawrence."

"Emma's brother?"

"That's right."

He could see the resemblance now. Edward was about twenty-four or twenty-five, the middle child between the oldest, Emma, and the youngest, Melissa.

The two men shook hands.

"What brings you here?" Edward asked.

"I'm trying to take your sister on a picnic."

"Excellent!" Edward said. "I don't think she's ever been on one before."

"Have you?"

"Of course," he said. "I've taken many girls on picnics. You see, I'm not like my sister."

"In what way?"

"I don't believe that I have to make my own way," Edward said. "I'm perfectly happy spending my father's money."

"And who is your sister Melissa like?" Clint asked. "You or Emma?"

"Oh, Melissa's like me, but she also gets men to spend *their* money on her. You see, Melissa is the pretty one in the family."

"I think Emma's very pretty."

"She is," Edward said, "but Melissa knows how to do the things women do to bring out their beauty. Emma— well, it's almost as if she tries to hide it."

"I see."

"If Emma ever took her hair *down* I'd be shocked," Edward said. "Oh, well, I guess I'll leave you to your picnic."

"You seemed to be in a hurry when you got here," Clint said.

"I was just going to ask my big sister to have lunch with me."

"Would you like to join us?"

"Oh, no," Edward said. "Like I said, I've been on picnics before. I know a third wheel is not wanted. Emma and I can have lunch another time. In fact, don't even mention that I was here."

The two shook hands.

"I'm sorry I wasn't at dinner last night, but I just got back from Elsah today. That's why I wanted to see Emma. I miss her when I'm away."

"If you really want to have lunch with your sister I can leave the basket—"

"No, no," Edward said, "I insist. You take Em on a picnic. I'll see if Melissa wants to have lunch, if I can find her."

"She wasn't at dinner last night, either."

"I know," Edward said. "Mother told me. It's more than likely she was off with one of the boyfriends our father disapproves of."

Edward turned abruptly and headed down the steps, then turned again before he reached the bottom.

"Have a nice picnic!" he called out and ran off.

At that moment Emma came out of the library.

"Was that my brother?"

"It was," Clint said. "Seems he wanted to have lunch with you."

"Where's he going?"

"To find Melissa," Clint said. "He didn't want to interfere with our picnic. We are going on our picnic, aren't we?"

"Oh, yes," she said, smiling, "we are definitely going on a picnic."

TWENTY-ONE

Clint had brought along a buggy he had rented from the hotel. He was also armed with directions to several likely places for picnics.

"You came well prepared," Emma said in the buggy.

"Well," he said, "I don't know the area, and you said you've never been on a picnic. I needed help."

"This will give us a chance to talk," she said.

"About what?"

"About the things I've read about you."

"Emma—"

"I won't pry, the way my father tried to do last night," she promised, "but I am . . . interested. How many of the things I've read are true?"

"Hardly any."

"Really?" She looked disappointed. "From what I read you're just as . . . wellknown as your friends Bat Masterson and Wyatt Earp. I also read you were good friends with Wild Bill Hickok."

"I had the honor of his friendship," Clint confirmed, "and the friendship of many others like Bat and Wyatt."

"And Doc Holliday?"

"I know Doc."

"All these . . . notorious men are your friends, so . . ."

"So I must be notorious, as well?" he asked.

She looked away, embarrassed.

"Look, Emma," Clint said, "most of the things you've read about me and all these other men, they're . . . exaggerated accounts of things that probably did happen."

"Like the O.K. Corral?"

"Yes, like that. Most of the time we're just normal men trying to live normal lives . . . and then along comes somebody—usually some young man—who's read all that garbage, and has believed it, and wants to prove he's faster than me or Wyatt or Doc, and we have to kill to keep from being killed."

"That must be terrible for you," she said.

"It is," he said. "Believe me, I try to avoid trouble as much as I can, but when forced into it . . . I defend myself. No more, no less."

She put her hand on his arm and squeezed it gently.

"I'm sorry," she said. "I won't mention any of the material I've read again."

"Just get to know me," he said, "the man who is right here in front of you. That's all I ask. Judge me then."

"All right," she said. "Now, where is one of these picnic spots?"

TWENTY-TWO

They found that the first place they drove to suited both of them. There was grass and trees, and they could see the river from where they were.

"This is lovely," she said as Clint helped her down from the buggy.

"Wait," he said. "I'll get the blanket."

He reached into the back of the buggy and took out a blanket the hotel had given him. He spread it out on the grass and then went to get the basket.

"Come and sit," he said, leading her to the blanket.

"This is so beautiful," she said, sitting opposite him on the blanket. "I feel so . . . guilty."

"Guilty? Why?"

"Because I'm not working."

"I couldn't help but notice," he said, "that your brother doesn't share your feelings about working for yourself."

"Oh, no," she said, "I love Edward dearly, but he loves the idea of being from a rich family. I don't know what he would do if he had to make his own way in the world."

"If you feel that way," Clint said, "why do you live in your father's house, even though you're out working for yourself?"

"Oh, I don't live there," she said.

"You don't?" he asked, surprised. "I thought, since you invited me there . . ."

"Oh, no," she said, "I just—well, I didn't invite you to my home because—well, I can't cook."

"That doesn't matter," he said. "Look." He reached into the basket and came out with a chicken leg. "See? You don't have to be able to cook to have food. Here."

He handed her the chicken and a napkin and then busied himself taking the rest of the food out of the basket. There was fruit, and some cheese, and some biscuits. Finally, he came out with the bottle of wine and two glasses.

"Mmmm," she said, putting the chicken leg down and picking up a piece of cheese. He poured the wine, and she accepted the glass from him.

"Sometimes I wish I could just eat the way they do in France," she said.

"And how is that?"

"Just cheese, bread, and wine."

"Well," he said, "here we have cheese, bread, and wine . . . and some chicken for me."

He took another chicken leg out and bit into it, then sipped his wine.

"So this is a picnic," she said.

"This is it."

She looked around, smiled at him, and said, "It's very nice."

"Yes, it is," he said. "There's nothing like fresh air, good food, good wine, and a lovely woman."

She blushed.

"You do know that you're lovely, don't you?"

"No," she said, waving the compliment away. "You wouldn't say that if you had met my sister Melissa last night. She's beautiful."

"So are you."

"Not like her," Emma said. "She's twenty years old and gorgeous."

"Emma—"

"I don't . . . I can't make myself look the way she does," Emma said. "I don't know how."

"I think you could learn very easily," he said. "I don't know anything about women's hair and using face paint, but I'll bet you could learn—but then, you really don't have to."

"I don't?"

"You look fine the way you are. I'm sure men are always asking you out to dinner or dancing."

She laughed and said, "No. Oh, I've had men show interest in me, but then they meet Melissa . . . and that's that."

"Your sister steals your boyfriends?"

"Oh," she said, "they're not boyfriends. They're never around long enough to become boyfriends. But they are men, and men like pretty things . . . like Melissa."

"And what does she do with them?"

"She goes out with them once or twice, lets them spend money on her, and then moves on to the next one. That's how Melissa does it."

"Does she try to steal these men from you?"

"Oh, no," Emma said. "My God, she doesn't have to *try*. They are just all over her from the minute they see her. She can't help it—and neither, I think, can they."

"So you don't blame anyone?"

"Who is there to blame?" she asked. "Except maybe myself, for letting it happen."

"You know," he said, leaning closer and lowering his voice, "I think when the right man comes along you won't *let* it happen."

"You think so?"

"I know so."

He poured more wine into their glasses and then held his aloft until she did, also.

"To the right man," he said.

"The right man," she repeated, and they drank.

TWENTY-THREE

They ate every bit of chicken, cheese, and bread the kitchen had given Clint, and they finished the bottle of wine.

"I don't have another bottle," he lamented.

"That's all right," she said, lying on her back. "That one's made me dizzy enough."

"Dizzy?" he asked. "On a half a bottle of wine?"

She laughed. "I said I loved wine, not that I could hold it," she said.

"Well, if I'd known that I would have made sure we had a second bottle," he said. He moved the basket so that he could lie on his back next to her.

"Is the Piasa bird the real reason you came to Alton?" she asked.

"It's the real reason."

"Why?" she asked. "I mean, why do you think you became fascinated by it?"

"Maybe because I had the time," he said. "Maybe because I wasn't going anywhere in particular when I saw it. I had the time to stop and admire it, and the time to wonder who painted it, and then the time to spend trying to find out."

"You're an extraordinary man."

"Why?" he asked. "Because I don't have a regular job—which, after all, is the real reason I have all this time to spend."

"Have you ever had a regular job?" she asked.

"You mean a job with regular hours and a regular paycheck? Not really. The only job I've ever really had was the law. I started as a deputy, then a sheriff. I've been a deputy marshal a time or two. Other than that, gunsmithing is all I know. So I guess the answer is no, I've never had a regular job like store clerk or bank teller."

"Do you think you could ever do those things?" she asked.

"Oh, no," he said, "not after all these years of doing whatever I want. I don't think I could ever work for somebody else now."

"So where do you get your money—if I may be so bold as to ask."

"I've put some money away," he said. "I've invested in some businesses over the years that put money in the bank for me, and I gamble fairly successfully—that is, when I gamble."

"You're a gambler?"

"Sometimes," he said. "Poker mostly."

"My father hates gambling."

"Well, then I guess he'll never consent to our marriage."

"What?" she asked, jerking her head his way.

He took her hand and said, "I'm kidding, Emma, just kidding."

"I knew that," she said, flustered.

They lay there together silently for a while, and Clint was thinking that if she was a different kind of woman he'd roll over now and kiss her.

"Do you think you ever will?" she asked.

"What?" He wondered if she'd somehow been reading his mind.

"Get married," she said. "Do you think you'll ever get married?"

"Oh," he said, "no."

"Just . . . no?"

"I don't think I'll ever get married," he said. "The answer is no."

"Why not?"

"I'm too old."

"You are not!"

"I mean, I'm too old and set in my ways to start considering someone else," he said. "Also, I don't think I could stay in one place very long."

"I see." After a few moments she asked, "How much longer do you think you'll be in town?"

"I don't know." In truth if it was just the Piasa bird keeping him here, he'd give it another day and then give up on it. However, now the police wanted him to stay around for a while.

"Emma," he said, "there's something I have to tell you."

"What?"

He raised himself up and propped his head on his arm so he could look down on her.

"There may be some policemen talking to your father about me."

"Police? Why?"

"Well . . . I was in Elsah before I came to Alton, and someone I talked to there has been killed."

"Oh, my God, who?"

"A woman."

"And do they think that you had something to do with it?"

"Well, they might."

"Why?"

"The woman and I had a sort of argument."

"About what?"

"I called her skinny," he said, "and she didn't like it."

"And they think you'd kill her over something like that?"

"I'm not sure what they think, but I had to tell them where I was last night. They'll probably be talking to your father and then to you."

"Well, I'll tell them you never could have killed anyone . . ."

Suddenly he knew she was thinking about his reputation.

"You see?" he said. "That's another problem with having all those things written about me."

TWENTY-FOUR

When they got back to town, Emma told Clint to drop her off at the library. Again, if she'd been another kind of woman he would have tried to get her to take him to her rooms.

In front of the library he got down from the buggy and helped her down. She had become quiet since he'd told her about the woman in Elsah.

"Is there anything you want to ask me?" he said before leaving.

"About what?"

"I don't know," he said. "About anything we discussed today."

"No," she said, "I don't think so."

"Okay, then," he said. "I'll talk to you . . . soon."

"Thank you for a lovely picnic," she said, and went up the stairs.

He watched her go inside and shook his head. Reading all those exaggerated stories about him had not upset her. What had? Was it that a woman he had known in Elsah had been killed, or was it that she thought he'd *known* this woman in Elsah? It was probably just as well that he hadn't told her about Amanda.

He got back into the buggy and drove it back to the hotel livery.

When he entered the hotel lobby he saw Detective Garrett waiting for him there, without his partner.

"Where's your silent partner?" he asked.

"He's out working."

"And what are you doing here?"

"Working."

"On the Elsah thing?"

"Is that the way you refer to the violent beating death of a young woman?" Garrett asked. "As a 'thing'?"

"Do you or do you not want to talk to me about something, Detective Garrett?"

"As a matter of fact, I do," the man said. "How about we do it over a cup of coffee?"

"Fine," Clint said. "Let's go into the dining room."

Clint led the way into the dining room. From the way the detective was eyeing it he'd never been in there before, either.

When they were seated Clint ordered a pot of coffee from the waiter.

"Anything with it?" the waiter asked the detective.

"Do you have pie?" the detective asked the waiter.

"Yes, sir."

"What kind?"

"All kinds," the bored-looking waiter said.

"Do you have rhubarb?"

"Yes, sir."

Garrett made a face and said, "I hate rhubarb. I'll have a slice of blueberry."

"Blueberry, yes, sir," the waiter said, then turned to Clint. "And you, sir?"

"Peach."

"Yes, sir. Coming up."

As the waiter walked away Garrett said, "I don't know how anybody can eat rhubarb."

"I happen to agree with you," Clint said. "Was there something else you wanted to talk about besides rhubarb pie?"

"I spoke with Mr. Lawrence today at his home."

"Is that a fact?"

"He confirmed what you told me about being at his home for dinner."

"Good."

"However," Garrett said, "he denied that you were friends. In fact, he said that was the first time he'd ever met you."

"And here I thought we'd made friends," Clint said, shaking his head. "Well, I guess I'm really more a friend of his daughter."

"Yes, well, he told us his daughter worked at the library," Garrett said. "We went over there to talk to her, but she wasn't there. They told us she left with a man fitting your description."

"That was me," Clint said, nodding. "We went on a picnic. She's back there now, though, in case you want to talk to her."

"Well, actually," Garrett said, "that's where my partner is. We decided that he'd talk to her and I'd talk to you again."

The waiter came at that point with their pie, and they waited while he set them down and walked away.

Garrett tasted his and sat back, savoring it.

"That's the best blueberry pie I ever had."

Clint had to admit that the peach was pretty good, as well.

"Did you want to double-check my story?" he asked.

"I guess you could say that was what I was doing," the detective said. "But I don't think you're about to change it."

"That's because it's true."

"For whatever reason. I know your reputation, Mr. Adams."

"It's not exactly a secret."

"No, it's sure not. You know, just between you and me, I don't think you killed that girl."

"Well, thanks . . ."

"My partner does, though," Garrett went on.

"Why?"

"Well, I believe it has something to do with the scraped knuckles of your left hand."

Clint looked at the offending hand. He still couldn't remember how he'd scraped it or where.

"I suppose if you could come up with a logical explanation for that it would help—but my partner's not the only one who thinks you did it."

"Who else?"

"The sheriff in Elsah."

"That doesn't surprise me," Clint said. "He was stuck on the girl."

"You say you had a run-in with some of her boyfriends?" Garrett asked.

"Yep. I get the feeling she had a lot, though I can't see it myself."

"You don't like skinny women?"

"I can like any kind of woman, Detective, but this one had an attitude."

"I see," Garrett said, "an attitude that you didn't like."

"No, I didn't like it," Clint said, "but I don't kill somebody when I don't like their attitude."

"When do you kill somebody, Mr. Adams?" Garrett asked. "I mean, just so I know."

"When I'm threatened with being killed myself, Detective."

"Sheriff Blaine said something about you almost shooting an unarmed man in Elsah. Now, what was that all about?''

Clint took a deep breath and let it out.

''That was one of the girl's boyfriends, a big brute about six and a half feet tall. She convinced him that he had to hurt me to prove his love. I wasn't about to be hurt.''

''So you would have shot him?''

''Damn right I would have,'' Clint said. ''He could have killed me by accident, just because he was trying to prove his love.''

Garrett finished the last of his pie, washed it down with some coffee.

''What was this brute's name?''

''Nate . . . something. Everybody in town seemed to know who he was.''

Garrett stood up. ''I'll check on him.''

''I'd appreciate it.''

''Oh,'' Garrett said, before leaving, ''have you found any information on that painting you were interested in?''

''No, nothing.''

''Too bad,'' Garrett said. ''Well, thanks for your time, Mr. Adams . . . and thanks for the pie.''

''Glad I could be of service.''

Garrett waved and left the dining room. Clint poured himself another cup of coffee and sat back. Was Garrett telling the truth when he said he didn't think Clint had killed Ellie? Or was that just some sort of ruse to throw him off guard?

Well, it didn't matter, really, because he hadn't killed the girl. The detective could try all he wanted to catch an innocent man off guard; it couldn't be done.

TWENTY-FIVE

Clint never made it back to his room.

As he left the dining room and walked past the front desk, the clerk called out to him by name.

"Yes?"

"There's a man waiting to see you, sir," the clerk said. Another policeman? he wondered.

"Where?"

"Right over there, sir," the clerk said, inclining his head.

Clint turned and saw a dapper-looking man in a suit sitting on one of the lobby sofas. He walked over to him.

"Are you looking for me?"

The man stood up quickly. He was several inches shorter than Clint and about ten years younger. He had a bowler hat tucked beneath his arm.

"Are you Mr. Clint Adams?"

"That's right," Clint said. "Who are you?"

"My name is of no importance, sir," the man replied, "but it is Clark, Matthew Clark."

"Do I know you, Mr. Clark?"

"No, sir," the smaller man said, "but you know my employer."

"And who might that be?"

"Wendell Lawrence."

"I do know Mr. Lawrence. Did he send you here?"

"He did."

"Why?"

"He would like to see you."

"When?"

"As soon as possible."

"Like now?"

"If now would be convenient," Clark said, "I have a buggy outside."

Clint thought about it for a moment and then said, "Sure, why not? Let's go."

The man led him to a buggy outside and drove him not to Wendell Lawrence's home but to a building in what Clint supposed was the business district of Alton.

He followed Clark to the second floor of the building and down a hall.

"Does Mr. Lawrence have this whole floor?" Clint asked the man.

"There are five floors in all," Clark said, "but Mr. Lawrence owns the entire building."

They went to an unmarked door, which Clark opened with a key. When they passed through Clint found himself in a waiting room with a woman seated at a desk. There was another door, which Clint assumed was used by the public. Why Clark felt the need to use this door was beyond him. Probably having the key gave the smaller man a feeling of power.

"This is Mr. Adams, Mrs. Fox."

Mrs. Fox was a handsome woman in her early fifties, approximately the same age as Mrs. Lawrence.

"You may go right in, Mr. Adams," she said. "He's ready for you."

"Thank you, Mrs. Fox." He turned to Clark. "Are you coming?"

"No, sir," the man said. "My job is finished."

"And you did it very well, too, Mr. Clark."

"Thank you, sir. Please, it's best not to keep Mr. Lawrence waiting."

Clint turned, opened the door, and went in. Wendell Lawrence was sitting at a huge desk that had a gleaming top. Clint knew it was gleaming because there was nothing on it: no papers, no files, no pencils or inkwells. Nothing.

"Ah, Mr. Adams," Lawrence said. "Good of you to come. Please, sit down."

Clint sat in a chair right across from Wendell Lawrence.

"For a busy man you keep a clean desk."

"Actually," Lawrence said, "my office is on the top floor. I use this one to see people. You wouldn't believe the mess upstairs."

Clint thought he would, but he kept quiet.

"Why did you ask me to come here, Mr. Lawrence?" he asked.

Lawrence made a steeple out of his fingers and peered at Clint over it.

"I had a visit from a Detective Garrett," Lawrence said.

"I'm aware of that."

"Apparently he's conducting some sort of murder inquiry, and you are involved."

"Not involved, actually," Clint said. "I met the dead girl once."

"Really?" Lawrence asked. "Hmm, I had the distinct impression that you were . . . suspected of this terrible crime."

"Did Detective Garrett say I was suspected of anything?" Clint asked.

"Not in so many words," Lawrence said. "No, I simply got the feeling . . . that he was hinting."

"And now," Clint said, "you want me to stay away from your daughter."

Lawrence smiled. "I knew you were a smart man, Mr. Adams," he said. "Yes, I want you to stay away from her—far away. To that end I am willing to pay you ten thousand dollars to . . . go away."

"Ten thousand," Clint said. He whistled soundlessly. "That's a lot of money just to go away."

"I don't know what you did in Elsah and I don't care," Lawrence said. "I just don't want my daughter involved with you."

"Mr. Lawrence," Clint said, "I didn't do anything in Elsah, but to take your ten thousand dollars and go away would sure make it seem like I did. I'm afraid I can't take you up on your offer."

"I can increase my offer."

"For all I know," Clint said, "you've got Detective Garrett or his partner, Detective Stevens, in the next room listening, and the minute I took your offer they'd jump out and arrest me."

"That's . . . preposterous."

"So is offering me money to go away, just to get me away from your daughter."

"I'm only trying to protect her."

"Maybe you think you're being a good father," Clint said. "I can't judge you for that. But I'm not interested in your money."

"With my money or without," Lawrence said, "I would advise you to leave town. It would be in your own best interest."

"That sounds like a threat, Mr. Lawrence."

"I should tell you that I'm not afraid of you, Mr. Adams, or your reputation. You see, I have enough money to overcome anyone's reputation."

Lawrence was rather typical of the wealthy men Clint had known. They all thought that money was power.

"I think this meeting is over, Mr. Lawrence," Clint said.

"Remember what I said, Adams."

"And remember what I say, Lawrence," Clint replied, standing up. "If anyone comes after me and I find out that you paid them I'll be coming for you."

"Now that sounds like a threat," Lawrence said. "I can have you arrested for that."

"It's not a threat, it's a promise, Lawrence," Clint said. "Your money won't protect you from me."

"I think you should leave."

"I'm already gone," Clint said and went out the door.

"You were wrong," he said to Mrs. Fox, in the waiting room.

"About what?"

"He wasn't ready for me at all."

TWENTY-SIX

After Clint left, Wendell Lawrence walked to the door, opened it, and stuck his head out.

"You can come in, Gina."

Gina Fox stood up and followed Lawrence into the office. She closed the door behind her.

"What was that about?" she asked.

Lawrence undid his tie, kicked off his shoes, and said, "I think I'm going to need you to contact Mr. Dillon for me."

"Oh, no, Wendell," she said, "not him."

He discarded the tie and took off his jacket, hanging it on the back of his chair.

"I thought we were beyond using men like him," she said.

"So did I, dear Gina," he said, "but that was before a man like Clint Adams came into our lives."

He removed his shirt and undid his trousers, dropping them and his underpants to the floor.

"Come here."

"Wendell . . ."

"Come here like a good girl."

Far from a girl, Gina Fox, though vibrant and attractive,

was fifty years old. Still, she could not resist her boss, had never been able to resist him, not in the entire twenty years she'd worked for him.

She got on her knees in front of him and began to tease his penis erect with her tongue.

"Ah, Gina . . ." he said, reaching for her head.

It was very soon after his marriage that Wendell Lawrence realized that his wife was never going to be able to satisfy him sexually. Luckily, at that point in time, he was already having a sexual relationship with another woman who worked for him. When his wife found out about it, he dismissed the woman and promised it would never happen again—but that was before he hired Gina Fox to work for him. Now he and Gina had been having sex for twenty years. He didn't know if his wife knew about it or not, but he suspected she had stopped caring a long time ago. He could count on one hand the times they'd had good sex together during their marriage. Ellen was just too cold, and Lawrence had passions she knew nothing about.

Gina Fox took his penis into her mouth and began to suck him. He didn't know why, but it excited him when she did this and kept all her clothes on. It had nothing to do with her body—which was lovely, with breasts still firm and skin still smooth and fragrant—but there was something about *this* situation that simply excited him.

Whenever they had sex it was always in this office. Never upstairs. Never in a bedroom, anywhere. More often than not he'd taken her right here on this desk. Today, however, she was giving him just what he wanted, what he needed. He kept his hands on her head as she bobbed back and forth, his slick penis sliding in and out of her mouth. When she felt his legs trembling from the impending explosion, she quickened her pace, and when he groaned out loud and began to ejaculate she stopped moving her head and simply sucked on him until he was dry. . . .

She stood up then and dabbed at her lips with her hand.

"When do you want to see Dillon?" she asked, her eyes shining. Gina always took great satisfaction from knowing that while she was sucking her boss's penis his wife was probably at some woman's club meeting or some charity function. Once they all went to a charity function together, and Wendell had pulled her into a closet, hiked up her dress, and taken her right there and then. Later she sat across from his wife with his juices still oozing from between her legs. . . .

"I want to see him first thing in the morning in this office," Lawrence said, pulling his pants up.

"Just him?"

"Just him," Lawrence said. "But when you contact him tell him that this job will probably require more than one man."

"Yes, sir. Will that be all?"

"That will be all, Gina," Lawrence said with a satisfied smile. "Thank you, Gina."

"Yes, sir," she said, and left the office. When she got to her desk she dabbed at her mouth again, this time with a tissue.

Inside Lawrence finished buttoning his shirt, tied his tie, and put his jacket back on, then left to go up to his regular business office. Clint Adams would be forgotten for the remainder of the business day.

TWENTY-SEVEN

Clint made his way out of the building and realized he'd have to find his own way back to the hotel. Luckily the Stratford was up on a hill, and he was actually able to see it from where he was. He started walking toward it and was eventually able to find a cab to take him the rest of the way.

He wasn't sure what that had all been about. Had the detectives been in the next room? Or had this truly been about Wendell Lawrence trying to protect his daughter? Or was he trying to protect himself from some kind of scandal?

Clint knew the way wealthy men like Wendell Lawrence usually worked. They got somebody else to do their dirty work for them. He had the feeling he was going to have to watch his back the rest of the time he was in Alton.

By the time he reached his hotel he'd convinced himself that the police had nothing to do with the meeting. He simply didn't think it was Detective Garrett's style, and he didn't think Detective Stevens would do it without consulting with his partner.

As he entered the lobby he looked around, wondering if someone else was going to intercept him today or if he was finally going to make it to his room.

He made it.

But so did someone else.

When Clint opened the door he smelled the perfume. Since he hadn't had a woman in his room—yet—the rest was pretty obvious.

"I'll bet," the girl said from the bed, "you've found a lot of women in your bed over the years."

"A few," he said. "Most of them I knew. You I don't."

"Does it matter?" she asked. "I'm naked, and I'm ready. Isn't that the way men like their women?"

"I like mine," Clint said, turning up the lamp, "introduced." He took a good look at her and added, "And older. Hello, Melissa."

She pouted, pulled the sheet up to her neck as if she was cold.

"How did you know?"

"You look like your sister."

"Oh, please," she said, "I must be having a bad day."

"Not at all," Clint said. "You're just as beautiful as your sister and your brother said you were."

"Then why are you still dressed?"

"I just came from seeing your father."

"Really?" she asked. "What did dear old Dad have to say?"

"He told me to stay away from Emma. What would he say if he knew about this?"

"Nothing," she said. "Emma's his favorite, you know. He doesn't care what I do."

"Which, I suspect, is the very reason you do most of the things you do, isn't it?"

"Probably."

"You'd better get dressed, Melissa."

"Don't you want to see what's under the sheet?"

"I'll wait for you downstairs. I'll buy you a cup of coffee, and we can get acquainted."

"You don't know what you're missing."

"I'll take that chance," he said and left the room. Well, at least he'd gotten to it, even if he hadn't been there very long.

Melissa came down in half an hour. Apparently, it had taken her that long to put herself together again. When she entered the dining room he saw how truly beautiful she was. She had long dark hair; eyes like a cat; a big, wide, sensuous mouth; and full, round breasts. She was shorter than Emma, probably about five four. Clint couldn't remember when he'd seen a more vibrant, beautiful young woman.

"What's wrong?" she asked when she reached the table.

"I'm actually sorry now that I didn't at least take a peek under the sheet."

She gave him a smile he was sure had melted the hearts of many men and said, "Now that was a sweet thing to say."

Three waiters came over, practically panting, and asked if they could help.

"You," Clint said, picking one. The other two skulked away. "Coffee."

"And for the young lady?"

"I'll have coffee, too," she said, giving the man a smile.

"Yes, miss. Right away."

"Are you actually used to having this effect on men?" he asked.

"Not on all men, I see," she said, looking at him. "Emma didn't tell me how good-looking you were. She says she doesn't judge men by their looks."

"And you do?"

"That's the way they judge me."

"The foolish ones, maybe."

She sat back and stared at him. She was actually wearing a rather sedate dress, much like the one her sister had worn the night before at dinner, but on Melissa it looked sexy.

"You are a dangerous man, aren't you?"

"How so?"

"You seem to know what to say to women."

"I usually try the truth."

"That makes you a very rare man, indeed."

"You seem to be a very intelligent young lady."

"I am," She said. "Does it bother you that I'm so young?"

"Twenty, is it?"

"Yes."

"Your father seems to think I'm too old for Emma," Clint said. "What would he think of this?"

"I told you," she said. "He doesn't care."

"Maybe you're not giving him the benefit of the doubt," he said.

"He tried to buy you off, didn't he?"

"Yes."

"He does that with everyone. How much did he offer you?"

"Ten thousand."

"That's my weekly allowance."

"He offered to up it."

"If you did what?"

"Took it and went away," Clint said. "Stayed away from Emma."

The waiter came with their coffee, took his time putting it down and filling Melissa's cup.

"Thank you," she said without a smile.

"If there's anything else I can do—"

"There is," she said. "Go away."

"Yes, miss."

Melissa looked at Clint. "Are you in love with my sister?"

"Not at all," Clint said. "I like her."

"But you wouldn't take the money."

"To take the money and leave would make me look guilty."

"Of what?"

He told her.

"You're right," she said, "it would make you look guilty—and my guess is you aren't."

"Why not?"

"Because if you were you would have taken it."

"What will your father do now?" Clint asked.

"He'll take steps to keep you away from his little angel."

"He'll send someone after me."

"Oh, yes," she said. "Most likely a man called Dillon."

"Dillon?"

She nodded.

"He's the man my father uses for his dirty work. Daddy doesn't know I know about Dillon."

"And how do you?"

She smiled. "Dillon saw me one day at the office. He came looking for me."

"And?"

"We sort of became . . . acquainted."

"Well acquainted?"

"Very well acquainted."

Well, there was no secret about what that meant.

TWENTY-EIGHT

"Well," she said after the coffee was gone, "you've met the whole family now. What do you think?"

"Well, I like everyone but your father."

"You like my mother?"

"Yes, I do. I think she's a very fine and attractive woman."

"If I couldn't interest you in me, maybe I can interest you in my mother?"

"I think all of the Lawrence women are charming, Melissa," he said, "but I don't think I'm ready to settle down. Besides, your mother loves your father."

"She does, actually, in her own way. But my father . . ."

"What about him?"

"Well, if you saw him at work today then you saw Gina Fox."

"His secretary?"

"She's more than that."

"How do you know?"

"Believe me," she said, "I know. Gina and I don't get along. She *knows* I know, and she rubs it in all the time, but subtly."

Clint conjured up the memory of Mrs. Fox and could see

what Melissa meant. There was something sensuous about the woman, even just sitting there in the office. Also, her manner had definitely said, "I belong here."

"I see you know what I'm talking about."

"Melissa," he said, "why did you come to my room?"

"I wanted to meet you," she said. "My mother and sister talked about you, and Emma told me about some of the things she read. I have to say, you're not at all how I thought you would be."

"How was that?"

"I thought," she said, "that when you saw me in your bed you'd just jump in after me."

"Sorry to disappoint you."

"Actually," she said, eyeing him curiously, "I told you that you didn't know what you were missing, but now I'm wondering what I'm missing."

"There are plenty of men out there your age."

"Oh, please," she said, "I don't think I've ever been with a man my age. I lost my virginity to a business associate of my father's when I was thirteen. I've been with older men ever since."

"Does your father know about that?"

"I've always thought," she said, "that my father set it up. I think the man told my father he wanted me, and my father used me to seal a deal."

"If I thought that was true . . ."

"It is," she said. "My father will do anything to close a deal, and he's always had little or no regard for me."

"Why is that?"

"Just between you and me?" she said. "I don't think he thinks I'm his."

"Has your mother ever been—"

"No," she said, "never, but since he has, I'm sure he suspects her."

Suddenly, Clint just wanted to hold Melissa in his arms, the way you'd hold a child. If she had lost her virginity at thirteen and then went on from there, she probably didn't have much of a childhood.

"Now I've done it," she said.

"Done what?"

"You feel sorry for me."

"I . . ."

"See. You can't deny it. You want to make me feel better, don't you?"

"Yes," he said truthfully.

"Good," she said, "then let's go back to your room."

"No."

She frowned at him. "I can't remember the last man who said no to me."

"Maybe it's about time somebody did."

She thought that over and then said, "No, I don't think so. I don't think I like it." She stood up.

"Melissa—"

"I have to go, Clint. Can I at least call you Clint?" she asked.

"Sure, you can."

"Be careful of my father," she said. "He's sure to send Dillon after you."

"What's Dillon look like?"

"Dark, about thirty-five," she said. "Dangerous-looking."

"I'll remember."

"You do that. I wouldn't want to see anything happen to you. I haven't given up on you yet."

"Melissa."

"Yes?"

"Do you live at home with your parents?"

"Oh, yes," she said. "I'm determined to make my daddy pay for my room and board just as long as I possibly can."

"Do you get along with your brother? And your sister?" he asked.

"I know I sound jealous of Emma," she said, "but I love my brother and my sister, and I love my mother very much. My father is the only one whose grave I'm looking forward to dancing on."

As she walked away Clint couldn't help thinking that she was entitled to dance on the grave of a man who would pimp her out at thirteen just to close a business deal.

TWENTY-NINE

Melissa Lawrence found herself liking Clint Adams, but she didn't like the fact that he had resisted her. In fact, it bothered her enough to go looking for Dillon that night. She knew her father would be sending for him, and she knew where he drank when he was in town. She walked into the Green Ripper Tavern that night, wearing one of her lower-cut dresses, showing off her firm, round breasts. She attracted all eyes when she entered, and men even started cutting cards for the right to go after her. They didn't get the chance, though, because Kevin Dillon spotted her as soon as she walked in, walked up to her and grabbed her arm.

"What the hell are you doin' here, little girl?" he demanded.

She smiled, licking her lips lasciviously, and said, "Looking for you, big boy."

Kevin Dillon was a big man, over six feet, very solidly put together. She'd been telling the truth when she told Clint Adams that he was dangerous-looking, but the very same scar that ran down the right side of his face which made him look that way also made him look sexy. She knew women wanted him, but she also knew that he wanted her. When she was around no other woman had a chance.

"Let's get out of here," he said, "before you get your-self—or me—killed."

He pulled her out the door and they started down the street.

"How many times have I told you the riverfront is not the place for you?"

"What are you, my father?" she demanded.

He stopped her, grabbed her by the arms, pulled her to him and kissed her. While he kissed her he pulled the top of her dress down so that her breasts bobbed free and he squeezed them.

"Your father ever do that to you?" he asked, releasing her.

She pulled her dress back up over her breasts and said, "That's about the only thing he hasn't done to me."

"Come on," he said, grabbing her again, "let's go to my hotel."

Kevin Dillon had Melissa Lawrence naked on his hotel bed, on her hands and knees, and he was driving his rigid penis into her from behind. He'd never known a woman—a girl, really, because she was still only twenty—who had the sex-ual appetites that she had. He knew nothing of the things she had told Clint that afternoon because when they got together they usually just fucked and rarely—if ever—talked.

Melissa grunted every time Dillon drove into her, as she met each of his thrusts with one of her own. She closed her eyes, reveling in the way he filled her. Right or wrong she'd had sex with that man when she was thirteen, and ever since then she couldn't get enough of it.

Suddenly, Dillon roared and exploded inside of her and she was disappointed. She hadn't come close to reaching her climax yet, and she knew that now that Dillon was done

she wasn't going to. Big, tough, sexy-looking man couldn't
even satisfy her every time.

She rolled over onto her back, just about spitting his cock
out as she did.

"God," he said, staring down at her, "you're a beautiful
kid."

"Not a kid any longer, Kevin," she reminded him.

"No," he said, "I guess you're not that sixteen-year-old
anymore."

That was when they had first met, when she was sixteen
and he had done his first job for her father. He'd come to
the house, and that night she'd gone to his hotel and they
had fucked all night in his room. He satisfied her that night,
and the chance that it might happen again kept her coming
back. She thought about Clint Adams then. She was willing
to bet his women were always satisfied. She wondered if
he'd fucked her sister yet, then dismissed the thought. Not
Emma, who was still a virgin at twenty-seven.

"How'd you know I was in Alton?" he asked.

"I figured my father would send for you."

"Why's that?" He dropped onto the bed next to her,
lying on his back. His big hand rested on her thigh. She
reached for it and pushed it between her legs so that his
long, strong fingers were stroking her. She knew that he
was doing it absently, though, with no intent to satisfy her.

"I know what the job is that he wants you for."

"And how would you know that?"

"Because I've met him."

"A man?"

"Yes."

"Did you sleep with him?"

"I offered," she said. "He turned me down."

Dillon laughed uproariously.

"Wow, that must have made you mad."

"It did, at first, but he turned out to be a very nice man.
My father wants you to kill him."

"Why?"

"To keep him away from my sister."

"He turned you down, and he's after your sister?"

"Not that way," she said. "They're just friends."

"Sure," Dillon said, "I'd like to be friends with your sister, too. She still got her cherry?"

"You stay away from my sister," she said, digging her nails into his thigh.

"Jealous, huh?"

She wasn't, but she let him think she was. Actually, she just didn't want his dirty hands on Emma. Her older sister wouldn't know what to do with a man like Kevin Dillon— or a man like Clint Adams.

"So who's this fella your daddy wants to keep away from his daughter?"

"You ever hear of Clint Adams?"

His fingers stopped stroking her and he sat up straight.

"The Gunsmith?"

"I think that's what Emma said they call him."

"The Gunsmith is in Alton?"

"He's at the Stratford."

"Well, I'll be goddamned."

"So you know who he is."

"Who don't know who he is?" Dillon said. "The Gunsmith. Goddamn!"

"Are you willing to go after him for my father?" she asked.

"Shit," Dillon said, "I'd go after him for goddamned free!"

"Why?"

"Do you know the reputation the man who kills the Gunsmith would have?"

She rolled her eyes and said, "He'd be the man who killed the Gunsmith. So?"

"Hell, girl," Dillon said, "I know men would kill a

dozen times—a hundred—for a chance at a reputation like that.''

She sat up and swung her feet to the floor, reached for her underwear.

''I don't think I'll ever understand men.''

Kevin Dillon didn't hear her. He was still saying, ''The Gunsmith. Goddamn!'' over and over again.

''Maybe I'm wrong,'' she said, standing up and reaching for her dress. ''Maybe he doesn't want you to go after him, at all.''

''It don't matter,'' Dillon said, lying back down, lacing his fingers behind him. ''Like I told you, I'd do it for free.''

She pulled on her dress then looked down at him. She loved his body and wished he knew how to use it better.

''I have to go. Are you supposed to see my father tomorrow?''

''In the morning.''

''Well, I guess you'll find out then.''

''The Gunsmith,'' Dillon said, staring at the ceiling. ''Goddamn.''

''I'll let myself out,'' she said, and did. She didn't think he noticed that she'd gone.

THIRTY

Clint woke the next morning thinking about the Piasa bird. He was thinking that he was never going to find out any more about it than he already knew. He also thought about the feather in his saddlebag. What kind of bird could have lost such a large feather? A Piasa bird, surely—after all, it was supposed to be as big as a calf—but then, there was no such bird. It was just an Indian myth.

Wasn't it?

He got dressed and walked to the window to look out at Alton in the early morning. It was a cool, damp morning, and there was a fog floating over the Mississippi. If he was ready to forget about the Piasa bird he would have been leaving today, but for the police telling him not to.

He thought, then, about the saloon girl, Ellie. He'd found her abrasive and annoying, but a lot of men liked her. Still, there must have been another man out there who found her less than charming, because he had killed her in the most brutal fashion possible. As annoying as he had found her, he didn't think she had done anything to deserve that.

He looked down at his scraped left hand and wondered why he couldn't remember what had happened. Probably the only way to find out was to find the saloon he'd been drinking in that night, when he'd gotten directions from the doorman. He decided to go out, start following those same directions, and see where he ended up.

But first breakfast.

In the middle of breakfast Detective Garrett and Detective Stevens entered the dining room. Clint sat back, sighed, and watched them approach.

"Good morning," Garrett said.

"Morning, gentlemen."

"My partner's never been in here," Garrett said. "I told him how good the food was, so he wanted to try it. Mind if we join you?"

Clint's first inclination was to say no, but he quickly amended that and said, "Not at all. Have a seat."

Both detectives sat down. A waiter immediately appeared.

"What's good?" Garrett asked Clint.

"I'm having steak and eggs."

Garrett looked at the waiter and said, "Two steak and egg breakfasts."

"Don't you want to check with your partner first?" Clint asked.

"He usually lets me do the ordering."

Clint looked at Stevens, who said nothing.

"He doesn't think I did it anymore, does he?" Clint asked.

"Why would you say that?" Garrett asked.

"I don't know," Clint said. "It's just a feeling I have."

"Well," Garrett said, "let's just say he's not as convinced. If you could tell us how and where you scraped your hand, that would probably do it."

"I'm going to find that out today."

"Oh? How?"

"I'm going to try to retrace my steps from that night," Clint said. "I know I was buying a lot of drinks, and I must have drank a lot of them because I don't remember much after that.''

"That's pretty careless for a man with your reputation, isn't it?''

"Very careless,'' Clint said. "I'm not very happy about it, in fact.''

"I guess not.''

The waiter came then with two plates of steak and eggs and set them down in front of the detectives.

"I'm sorry,'' Clint said, "I'm afraid he made your steaks to my liking.''

"That's fine,'' Stevens said.

Only the second time Clint had heard him speak.

When the waiter had cleared their plates Clint ordered more coffee.

"Not for us, thanks,'' Garrett said, standing. "We have to get to work. We really appreciate the breakfast, though. It was great.''

"Don't mention it,'' Clint said. "I'm only sorry I hadn't extended the invitation myself.''

Stevens stood up and headed for the door.

"Is he married?'' Clint asked.

"Why, yes, he is.''

"Does he talk to his wife?''

"Of course.''

"And to you?''

"How could we work together if we didn't talk to each other?'' Garrett asked.

"I don't know,'' Clint said. "I guess it was just a silly question.''

"Well, again,'' Garrett said, "thanks for the meal.''

"There's something I think you should know, Detective Garrett.''

"What's that?''

"Wendell Lawrence offered me ten thousand dollars to get out of Alton."

"He did?"

"Yes."

"And you turned him down?"

"That's right."

"Why?"

"Because you told me not to leave."

Garrett rubbed his jaw. "I guess a guilty man would have taken the money, huh?" he said.

"Exactly."

"Or," Garrett said, "a guilty man would turn it down, hoping it would make him look innocent."

"You know," Clint said, "sometimes I wish you talked as much as your partner does."

"Why did he offer you this money?"

"He wants me to stay away from his daughter."

"The librarian?"

"That's right."

"Then he's just being a concerned father."

"I suppose so."

"Still . . . offering you money to leave, that's sort of interfering with our investigation."

"Sort of."

"Thanks for telling me," Garrett said.

"Don't mention it," Clint said. "I'm going to be here until you or Sheriff Blaine in Elsah find out who killed that girl."

"Blaine?" Garrett said and laughed. "He ain't gonna find out nothin'."

"So will you be going to Elsah to investigate?"

"I guess we'll have to," Garrett said. "They really do count on us for some things."

"Like murder?"

"I don't know," Garrett said. "This is the first one they've ever had. Good luck today, finding out where you scraped your hand. Let us know when you do."

"You'll be the first," Clint promised. "The very first."

THIRTY-ONE

Clint didn't know exactly what the two detectives were trying to tell him. Having breakfast with him—*on* him—could have been nothing more than trying to get a free breakfast. Clint wouldn't have put that past Garrett. His partner, however, for all his silence, conveyed a feeling of competence and seriousness. Maybe having breakfast with him for Stevens meant nothing more than, "I don't suspect you anymore."

He didn't know what Garrett was going to do with the information about Wendell Lawrence, either. Probably nothing, considering that Lawrence was an important man in Alton.

Clint paid the bill and left the dining room. It seemed to him all he'd been doing since he got here was buying other people drinks and meals—including the picnic with Emma. He had the feeling that, after that picnic, he wasn't going to hear from or see Emma again, as a result of her own choice. Maybe he just should have taken her father's money, then. What would the big difference have been?

He left the hotel and stopped right outside, replaying the conversation with the doorman from the other night. Broadway, the man had said, and pointed. Clint walked over to Broadway.

• • •

He found it by getting off Broadway, which he really didn't remember doing that night, but there it was, right on the corner of Broadway and Front. He remembered that all of the Broadway establishments had been pretty noisy, so he'd gone looking for something quieter. This place—which, no matter how hard he looked, seemed to have no name—had been quiet when he first walked in. He remembered two men bracing him for being a stranger in a saloon that obviously catered to a regular clientele, and recalled that buying drinks had gotten him off that hook. After that they had all liked him. So how had he ended up with scraped knuckles?

It was early and no amount of pounding on the door resulted in anyone answering it. He was just going to have to wait until the place was open—but at least he'd found it.

He'd accomplished something.

"Hello, Mrs. Fox," Dillon said as he entered the second-floor office.

She looked up and, with no expression, said, "Mr. Dillon. You can go right in. He's ready for you."

"Thank you, Mrs. Fox."

Melissa had told Dillon that Gina Fox was her father's mistress. "But they usually just do it in his second-floor office."

Despite the fact that Mrs. Fox was about fifteen years older than he was, Dillon wouldn't have minded giving her a tumble, himself.

He opened the door and entered the office.

"Dillon," Wendell Lawrence said from behind his spotless desk. "Glad you could come."

"Come on, Wendell," Dillon said. "You pay me well to come when you call. It's not like I have a choice in the matter. Not if I want your money lining my pockets."

"That's why we get along, Dillon," Lawrence said. "Because you know you want my money, and I know you want my money."

"Now, suppose you tell me what it is you want to give me your money to do?" Dillon said, seating himself.

"Do you know a man named Clint Adams?"

"Of course I know him," Dillon said, trying to act unimpressed. "They call him the Gunsmith."

"He's in Alton."

"And?"

"And I want you to get him out of Alton."

"That's all?"

"That's all. Oh, one other thing."

"Yeah?"

"How you do it is your business," Lawrence said. "I just want you to do it by the end of the week."

"This is gonna cost you."

"I'll pay you whatever you want," Lawrence said. "Just do it."

Dillon stood up. "Consider it done."

"Hire whatever help you need."

"I'll think about that and get back to you. If I do hire some help, it'll be you who pays them, not me."

"Fine. Just get the job done."

"Do you mind if I ask why?"

Wendell Lawrence smiled tightly. "The price goes down," he said, "if I have to explain why."

"Whatever you say, then," Dillon said. "You're the boss."

"Another reason why we get along, Dillon," Lawrence said. "Because you know that, too."

Dillon chuckled, said, "Yeah," and turned to leave the office.

THIRTY-TWO

Clint returned to the tavern—or saloon—when it opened at five p.m. The inside was deserted except for the bartender. Clint walked to the bar and stared at the man, but couldn't recognize him.

The bartender didn't have that problem, though.

"You!" he said. "I thought I told you not to come back here."

"Did you?" Clint asked. "I don't remember."

"It don't surprise me that you don't," the barman said. Clint noticed there was an abrasion on the point of the man's jaw.

"How did you get that?" he asked, pointing.

"Ha! Like you don't remember that, either?"

"Sorry, but I don't."

The bartender leaned his elbow on the bar and squinted at Clint.

"You was buyin' everybody in the house drinks, or don't you remember that?"

"That I do remember."

"And then you started matchin' 'em drink for drink."

"I don't remember that," Clint said. "I usually stick to beer."

"Well, believe me, you was downin' whiskey the other night."

"And then what?"

"And all hell broke loose," the man said, straightening up. "I had to close until I got this place put back together."

"A fight?"

"Ha! More like a riot. They was all fightin' over you like you was a dance-hall girl or somethin'—but all you was was a supply of free drinks."

"And you got hit?"

"It was you who hit me!"

Clint looked down at his scraped left knuckles.

"Would you tell a policeman that?"

"Now, why would I want to do that?" the man asked. "Was only a bar fight. I wouldn't wanta get you into trouble."

"No," Clint said, "if you'll tell that to a detective named Garrett you'd be getting me out of trouble."

The man stared at Clint, puzzled, then shrugged.

"Well," he said finally, "if that's what you want me to do, I'll do it. Got yourself in trouble with the law, did you?"

"For something I didn't do."

"Ain't that always the way?" he asked. "You want a beer?"

THIRTY-THREE

Before Clint left the tavern he asked the bartender for his name and the name of the place. The man said his name was Spike, and that the place had no name. He said to tell the police it was almost on the corner of Broadway and Front Street—sort of.

"Don't worry," Spike said before Clint left. "Any policeman should be able to find it."

Clint left the place and realized he didn't know where to find Detective Garrett. He went back to the hotel to see if anyone there knew.

"There's more than one police station, Mr. Adams," the desk clerk said. "Which one do you want?"

"I don't know. Look, never mind."

He remembered Garrett saying that he and Stevens might be going to Elsah. He was just going to have to wait for the two men to get in touch with him again—which, if recent history was any judge, wouldn't take too long. Once they talked to Spike about the bar fight he'd be free to leave Alton, the Piasa bird, Elsah, and the memory of a dead girl behind.

Kevin Dillon stood in a doorway across from the Stratford Hotel and watched Clint Adams enter. When he'd gotten there and asked for Adams, he was told he was out. A few bucks to the desk clerk had gotten him a description. He recognized Clint from it immediately. Clerks saw lots of people during the course of a day, and they were good at describing them.

Once Clint went into the hotel, Dillon walked across, mounted the hotel steps, and peered into the lobby. He saw Clint Adams walk past the desk clerk and up the stairs. Just to double-check he went into the lobby and up to the front desk.

"That was him," the clerk said.

"I figured," Dillon said. "What room?"

"I'm not supposed to—"

Dillon stopped him by putting money on the desk. It wasn't as much as Melissa Lawrence had given the man the night before to let her into Clint's room, but it was enough for him to give the man the room number.

"Okay," Dillon said, "thanks. Forget you saw me. Understand?"

The man cringed from the look in Dillon's eyes and said, "I understand."

"Good man."

Dillon turned and left the hotel.

In Elsah Detectives Garrett and Stevens were standing in Sheriff Rick Blaine's office. Garrett was thinking what a jerk Blaine was. Stevens was just staring at the sheriff, wondering why they were even there.

"You know," Garrett said, "this is, by all rights, your baby, Sheriff."

"I don't know nothin' about investigatin' no murder," Blaine said.

"That's obvious."

"What's that supposed ta mean?"

"Why did you decide Clint Adams was the killer?" Garrett asked.

"He argued with Ellie—with the girl."

"About whether or not she was skinny, right?"

Blaine hesitated, then said, "I guess . . ."

"And you think he'd kill her over an argument like that?"

"He probably decided he wanted to have sex with her and she refused him."

"Why would she do that?" Garrett asked. "We've been in town an hour and we already know she never refused anybody. Why would she refuse him?"

"Shit, I don't know."

"That's right, you don't know," Garrett said. "You don't know shit, that's why we're here to save your sorry ass."

"Now, look—"

"You look," Garrett said, "we got word that you were stuck on the girl."

"Well . . ."

"And so was a big guy called Nate something?"

"Tremayne," Blaine said, "Nate Tremayne."

"And she sent both of you after Adams for calling her skinny?"

Blaine didn't answer, but he fidgeted in his chair.

"We'll take that as a yes," Garrett said. "This town got a mayor?"

"Sure it does."

"How would he feel about his sheriff if he found out you tried to pin a murder on a man for calling your girl-friend skinny?"

"Now, look— "

"Never mind," Garrett said. "We'll pull your ass out of the fire on this one, Blaine, but I'm never coming back here after this."

He turned to Stevens, who was looking around the office. Garrett knew, though, that Stevens had taken in everything that had been said.

''Let's go to the hotel and find out who was in town that night,'' he said. ''That might tell us something.''

He looked at Blaine.

''We'll check in, Sheriff, before we leave town.''

''I—a-all right.''

''Let's go,'' Garrett said to Stevens, who led the way to the door.

''What a loser,'' he said outside.

''Yup.''

THIRTY-FOUR

Clint stayed in his room until early evening, when he got hungry. Initially he'd figured on staying in the hotel until Garrett and Stevens came looking for him. He was certain that Wendell Lawrence was going to send someone after him—whether it was somebody named Dillon or somebody else.

However, he'd come to change his mind. He'd never hidden from anyone before, and he wasn't about to start now. So he decided to go out and find someplace new to eat. Maybe he'd find himself a really fine meal before he left Alton for good.

Over dinner at a small café—which had attracted him because of the wonderful aroma emanating from it—he thought about where to go from here. He was too close to St. Louis not to stop there, so he made that decision pretty quickly.

The café served a beef stew that could only be described as great, and when he was done he was sorely tempted to order a second bowl. Instead, he wiped this one clean with the last of the biscuits, then ordered a slice of peach pie and another pot of coffee.

After dinner he decided to take a long route back to the hotel to walk the meal off. Deep down perhaps he hoped that Lawrence's man would make a try for him tonight. It seemed silly, really, to hire a man to hurt him or kill him, simply to keep him from Emma Lawrence. Now that he'd found out how he scraped his knuckles—and he was still upset with himself for getting so drunk he didn't remember it—he'd be leaving Alton pretty soon, anyway. Should he go and talk to Wendell Lawrence and tell him that? Or would that give the man too much satisfaction? Make him think that he had, in the end, forced Clint to leave town?

It was not an ego thing, but rather his intense dislike of the man that kept him from doing that. So he took the long way around, walking back to the hotel, and arrived safe and sound with no attempts to injure him or worse.

When he got back to the hotel he found Emma waiting to see him in the lobby. He decided they should probably put a special sofa there for people who wanted to see him, and give them numbers.

"Well," he said, approaching her, "this is either a co-incidence, or you came here to see me."

"It's not a coincidence, Clint," she said. "I-I'd like to talk to you."

"So talk."

"Somewhere private."

"The dining room?"

She ducked her head and said, "Even more private than that."

"My room, then," he said, "unless you're worried about your reputation."

"No," she said, "your room would be fine."

"Let's go, then."

THIRTY-FIVE

He allowed her to precede him, and directed her to his door.
As he unlocked it he wondered what she would think if she
knew that he'd found her sister in his bed the day before.
In fact, what would she think if they found Melissa there
now?

They didn't, of course. He unlocked the door, they entered, and he closed it behind them.

"What's this about?" he asked.

"I owe you an apology," she said.

"For what?"

"For the way I acted at the picnic."

"Or after the picnic."

"Yes," she said, "that's what I mean. After the picnic."

"After I told you about the dead girl."

She looked away and said, "Yes."

"What was the problem?" he asked. "Did you think I
was a murderer?"

"Of course not."

"A womanizer, then?"

She looked at him. "If you were," she said, "wouldn't
you have ... tried something ... by now?"

"With you?"

"Of course, with me."

"You're not that kind of girl, Emma."

She raised her chin and asked, "And what kind of girl am I, then?"

"A nice one."

She made a face. "I hate that," she said. "I hate being a nice girl. I'd rather be like—" She stopped short.

"Like Melissa?" he asked. "More like your younger sister?"

"Yes," she said, "I would like to be more like Melissa. Not exactly like her, but . . . to some extent."

"And you probably think she should be a little bit more like you."

"Yes," she said, "I think that would work. If you knew my sister—"

"But I do."

"What?" She was surprised. "When? Where?"

"I met her yesterday . . . here."

"Here? In your room?"

He decided not to be that honest.

"In the hotel," he said.

"What was she doing here?"

"She wanted to meet me," he said, "and, I think, warn me."

"About what?"

"Your father."

"Why would she want to warn you about my father?"

Clint told her about his meeting with her father, how the man offered him money to leave town and to leave her alone.

"That sounds like my father," she said when he was finished.

"I guess he was being concerned—"

"For himself, probably," she said. "For his reputation in Alton."

"Nothing wrong with that, I suppose."

"Don't defend him," she said. "He's always doing things like that. Trying to throw his money around to get his own way."

"You don't approve?"

"It's why I moved out, why I have my own place," she said. "It's why I want to make my own way. What else did Melissa tell you?"

"Let me think."

"Anything about me?"

"Oh, yes," he said, "she told me she loves you and your brother and your mother."

"But not Father?"

"No," he said, "not your father."

She bit her lip. "I disapprove of him, of course," she said, "but I haven't gone that far."

"Maybe you don't have reason to," Clint said, "and she does."

"Like what?"

"I suppose that would be for her to tell you."

"Did she say something to you?"

"Again," Clint said, "that's between you and her."

Emma sighed, walked to the bed, and sat down on it heavily.

"We're not close," she said. "I can believe she told you something she wouldn't tell me."

"Emma . . . why did you come here?"

"To talk to you."

"We could have done that downstairs," Clint said. "Why are you in my room?"

She looked up at him and then said, "Maybe I . . . want to go to bed with you."

"You came here to seduce me?"

"I . . . don't think I'd know how. I thought I'd just . . . ask you."

Offers from both of the Lawrence sisters in two days— and he was turning them both down.

"I'm afraid not."

"I'm not pretty enough?"

"You're very pretty."

"Are you afraid of my father?"

"No."

"Then why won't you take me to bed?"

"Because I think you're here for the wrong reasons," Clint said. "You're trying to prove something to yourself, and I don't think I want to be used that way."

"You're right," she said, standing up abruptly. "I've made a fool of myself. I'll leave—"

"Relax," he said, stepping in front of her. "You haven't made a fool of yourself. Don't be so hard on yourself."

"You're very nice, Clint," she said. "Thank you."

"For what?"

"For knowing what to do when I didn't."

"Emma," he said, "you think this over, and if you decide you still want to go to bed with me, I'll be right here."

"You mean . . . you do?"

"Definitely."

Suddenly, she looked very pleased with herself. Clint felt it was time to get her out of the room.

"Why don't I walk you downstairs?"

"A-all right," she said. "Thank you."

THIRTY-SIX

Kevin Dillon was again across the street, watching the Stratford Hotel, when Clint Adams came out with Emma Lawrence. Dillon immediately recognized Melissa's sister, his employer's older daughter. It was his job to get rid of Clint to keep him from being with Emma, and here they were coming out of the hotel together. To Dillon this meant one thing. They had already been together in Clint's room. If Lawrence found out about this, maybe Dillon wouldn't get paid, and wouldn't get his chance at Adams.

He knew he could go after Clint Adams on his own, but if he was going to do it he figured he might as well get paid for it. That would make taking the Gunsmith and making a name for himself even sweeter.

He watched as Clint put Emma in a cab and sent her off. They did not embrace or kiss, the way lovers would. Maybe he was wrong. Maybe they had been together but not for sex.

As the cab drove away Clint turned and went back into the hotel. Dillon still hadn't figured out how he was going to do his job. There was a nervous feeling in the pit of his stomach, which was to be expected. After all, this was the Gunsmith. The man's name was spoken in the same hushed whispers as those of Hickok, Earp, and Masterson.

Dillon rubbed his jaw. When he put it that way, he figured he probably would need some help.

Or, at least, some backup.

He stepped out of the doorway and started walking to the nearest telegraph office.

As Emma Lawrence walked from the cab toward her home, a man got out of another coach that was sitting right in front of her building. It was her father's man, Matthew Clark. She knew Clark to be a lackey, a stooge, even. She also knew that he lusted after her sister Melissa, but in that respect he was like every other man.

"Miss Lawrence?" He approached her as she headed for her door in the vain hope she could get to it before he got to her.

"What is it, Mr. Clark?" she asked, stopping short.

"Your father would like to see you."

"Where is he?"

"In the coach."

She almost asked, "Why doesn't he get out of the coach?" but she already knew the answer to that. Her father spent as little time as possible in public, and he hated walking the streets.

"Oh, all right."

"This way—"

"I know the way, Clark!" she said irritably.

"Yes, of course."

He hurried ahead of her, though, and held open the door of the coach.

"Emma," her father said, "get in. Clark?"

"Yes, sir?"

"Go for a walk."

"Er, how long a walk, sir?"

"I don't know."

"How will I know when to come back?"

"If we're gone when you get back," Lawrence said, "then your walk was too damn long."

"Uh, yes, sir."

Clark closed the door as Emma got in and went for his walk.

"Why does he take that kind of treatment from you?" she asked.

"He gets paid to."

"He could get another job."

"Don't be silly," he said. "What other job could he get that would pay him as well?"

She closed her eyes. There was no point in trying to discuss this with him.

"What did you want, Father?"

"I want you to stop seeing Clint Adams," Lawrence said.

"I see who I want to see, you know that."

"I know that, under normal circumstances, you enjoy doing whatever I tell you not to do, but this is different."

"How is that?"

"The man's a killer."

"Those are just stories—"

"The police came to see me about him," he said, interrupting her. "He killed a girl in Elsah."

"He did not."

"They say he—"

"I've talked to him about it, and he told me he didn't do it."

"And you believe him?"

"Of course."

"You're very naive, Emma."

"I know, Father," she said. "You've told me that many times."

"Will you stop seeing him?"

"I will see him as long as he wants to see me."

"Damn it—"

"I have to go."

He reached out and grabbed her arm.

"You're hurting me."

"You're going to get hurt a lot worse if you're around him when—"

"When . . . what?"

He released her and sat back, remaining silent.

"What did you do, Father?"

"I took steps to protect my family."

She stared at him a few moments and then said, "I have always thought you were a very foolish man."

"Emma—"

She opened the door and stepped out. She heard her father knock on the ceiling of the coach—his signal for the driver to go.

Clark was going to have to find his own way back.

THIRTY-SEVEN

Melissa Lawrence felt bad.

Of all the men she'd ever met, in ten minutes Clint Adams had affected her more than any of them. It was nothing sexual, he just seemed to be a very decent, nice man. Even the way Emma had spoken of him had made her envious of her sister's new friendship. She'd thought by taking him to bed she would accomplish something more than Emma had, but now she saw that she was wrong. Having sex with Clint Adams would not have brought her closer to him than Emma was.

She heard the key in the lock and then Emma entered and looked at her, not surprised, but somewhat resigned. She had long ago given Melissa her own key, but this was the first time she'd used it.

"Not you, too?"

"What do you mean?"

"I just talked to our father outside, in his coach," Emma said.

"About what?"

"He warned me to stay away from Clint Adams," Emma said.

"And?"

"I just came from seeing Clint. He told me he met you yesterday."

"Yes," Melissa said, wondering how much Clint had told Emma. "I went to his hotel."

"Why?"

"I was curious."

"Did you sleep with him?" Emma asked, folding her arms across her chest.

"No," Melissa answered, and then added, "I tried, but he rejected me."

Emma stared at her sister for several moments and then started to laugh.

"What's so funny?" Melissa asked.

"He rejected me, too, just a little while ago," Emma said. "I guess he's quite a man to be able to resist both of us."

"You were right about him."

"In what way?"

"He's . . . special. I mean, I only talked to him for half an hour or so, but you can see that."

"Yes," Emma said, "yes, you can. Melissa, I'm afraid our father may have done something foolish."

"He's sending Dillon after Clint."

"How do you know that?"

"I . . . I've seen Dillon."

"We have to warn Clint."

"Yes."

"Why did you see Dillon?" Emma asked. "You know how dangerous he is—wait, I know," she said quickly, as Melissa started to retort, "I sound like him, don't I?"

"Yes."

Emma shuddered. The last thing she wanted to do was sound like their father.

"What should we do?" she asked.

"Warn him!" Melissa said. "Against Dillon and who-ever he brings with him."

"He won't go after him alone?"

Melissa laughed. "He's wetting his pants to go after the Gunsmith alone," she said, "but he'll think better of it. He'll call for help."

"How many men?"

Melissa shrugged. "What do I know about these things?"

"You know Dillon," Emma said, "I assume you know him very well."

"Yes."

"Guess."

Melissa shrugged and said, "Three more."

"Four against one?"

"That seems about right."

"We have to warn him."

"We've established that. You have to go and warn him."

"Why me?"

"He's your friend," Melissa said, "and Dillon will probably have someone watching the Stratford, if he's not watching it himself."

"All right," Emma said, "I'll do it."

"You have to do it now, today," Melissa said, physically pushing her sister toward the door.

"All right, Melissa," Emma said, "I'm going."

"It would probably be better for him to leave Alton, but I doubt he'll do that."

"Not while the police are still investigating the death of that girl in Elsah."

"What girl?"

Briefly, Emma filled her sister in on what had happened in Elsah.

"Eddie just came back from Elsah," Melissa said of their brother. "I wonder if he knows anything that would help."

"All right, then," Emma said, "while I go and talk to Clint again, you find Edward and see if he knows anything."

"All right, then we'll leave together," Melissa said. "I think I know where Eddie will be."

They went out the door and down the stairs together and separated on the street after a brief but tight embrace.

THIRTY-EIGHT

It was getting dark and Clint was thinking of going out for a drink. He'd remained in his room since Emma had left, hoping the two detectives would come to talk to him, but they never showed up. They must've still been in Elsah.

He was reluctant to go down to the lobby. It seemed there was always someone there looking for him: first the police, then Lawrence's man Clark, then Emma. At least Melissa had been resourceful enough to get into his room.

How had she done that?

He decided to go down and find out.

"Can I help you, Mr. Adams?" the desk clerk asked.

This was the clerk who had checked him in, and the man who had been behind the desk when he found Melissa in his room yesterday.

"Yes," Clint said. "Yesterday evening when I returned to my room I found a girl there waiting for me. Can you tell me how she got there?"

To his credit the man didn't try to lie.

"She assured me that she was a friend of yours, sir, and that you'd be pleased to find her there. Indeed, had I found her in *my* room I would have been—"

"I know, overjoyed," Clint said. "I assume she tipped you for letting her in?"

"Well, sir," the man said, "we really don't make much money working here—"

"I don't care how much she gave you, just that she did give you some money—and I'm not looking to get you into trouble."

"Well, then, yes, sir, she did tip me."

"Good," Clint said. "Now tell me who else has given you money and asked questions about me in the last couple of days."

"Sir?"

"What's your name?"

"James, sir."

"You've been doing real well up to now, James," Clint said, "don't start to disappoint me."

"Sir, I wouldn't think of it."

"A man was in here looking for me."

"Yes, sir."

"He gave you some money."

"Yes, sir."

"You described me to him?"

"Yes, sir."

"And maybe even gave him my room number?"

"Uh—"

"James."

The young man had the good sense to avert his eyes and said, "Yes, sir."

"All right," Clint said, "I'm not going to give you any money, James, because I think you owe this to me. What did he look like?"

"He was big, dark, and scary-looking," the young man said, as if this would be his salvation. "I mean, he was *mean*-looking, you know?"

"I know," Clint said. "They're always mean-looking. One man?"

"Yes, sir."

"When?"

"Earlier today."

That was good. He probably had some time, then. If this was Dillon, he was going to need time to make up his mind how he wanted to handle the situation, whether or not he wanted to bring in other men. Clint felt sure that he *would* decide he needed help, and that would take some time, as well.

There was time.

"Okay, James," Clint said, "thanks."

"Uh, sir . . ."

"Don't worry," Clint said, "I'm not going to tell the manager."

"Thank you, sir." The young man was relieved.

"But I'd better not find anybody else in my room, no matter how beautiful they are."

"Yes, sir—I mean, no, sir. It won't happen again."

Clint nodded, then turned and saw Emma coming in the front door.

THIRTY-NINE

"You haven't changed your mind already, have you?" he asked.

He felt slightly foolish when she frowned at him, obviously not understanding what he said.

"What?" she said.

"Never mind."

"I came back to warn you."

"About what?"

"My father," she said. "He's sent a man named Dillon after you."

"I know," he said. "Melissa told me this yesterday."

"But I just saw my father," she said. "He's warned me to stay away from you or I could get hurt."

"Dillon was here."

"Already? You've seen him?"

Clint shook his head. "He paid the desk clerk to get my room number."

"You'll have to get out of the hotel."

"No," Clint said, "he was just checking to make sure I was here. He's not going to try for me in my room."

"Why not?"

"If he does that no one will know it was him," Clint

said. "He'll want to kill me where people can see. He wants that reputation."

"Well, Melissa knows Dillon, and she says he won't come without help."

"More likely backup than help," Clint said. "I figured that."

Now she gave him an exasperated look.

"If you have all this figured out, then why am I here?" she demanded.

He smiled and said, "Because you care, and I appreciate that. Where is your sister, by the way? Did she see your father, too?"

"No, she was waiting for me when I got home."

Clint—not knowing that Melissa had already confessed to trying to seduce him—refrained from making a remark about her breaking into people's rooms.

"Your father is right about one thing, though," he said instead.

"What's that?"

"You shouldn't be around me."

"Why don't you go to the police?"

"I want to, but right now I don't know where the two detectives are. Well, I do, actually—I think they're in El-sah."

"My brother just got back from Elsah."

"He must have been there when I was there," Clint said. "Maybe he knows something."

"That's what we thought, so Melissa is looking for him right now."

"It's nice to have both of you on my side."

"But not in your bed, huh?"

"What?"

"She told me you rejected her, too."

"I didn't reject either one of you," he said.

"What do you call it?"

He hesitated, then said, "Postponed."

"Both of us? So you expect to sleep with both of us before you leave?"

"No, of course not."

"Oh, so only one of us?"

"Yes—I mean, no—"

"Well, which is it? Yes? No? And which of us do you choose?"

"Emma—"

"Never mind," she said, putting up her hands. "I don't want to know. I'm going now. Just be careful, all right?"

"Yes, all right."

"I guess we can't very well fight over you if you're dead, now can we?" she asked, then quickly left.

"I guess not," he said to no one in particular.

FORTY

That night Kevin Dillon met with three men in a saloon down by the docks. It was not one that he frequented regularly, so no one was going to walk in and find him—like Melissa. He liked having her in his bed all right, but he didn't want her popping up in other parts of his life when least expected.

The three men were Mike Walden, Jack Borders, and Sam Barnes, and they were of a type: not very smart and willing to do anything for money. All were in their thirties and looked up to Dillon.

"What's the job this time, Dillon?" Walden asked.

"What's it pay?" Borders asked.

"That's all you care about, Jack," Dillon said. "Money."

"And women," Barnes said. "He cares about women."

"And it takes money to buy women," Jack Borders said.

"Well," Dillon said, "you'll be able to buy a lot of women after this job."

"Big pay?" Walden asked.

"Big pay."

"Why?" Barnes asked.

If any of them was a pessimist or had a suspicious nature, it was definitely Sam Barnes.

"Because the risk is high, Sam," Dillon said. "That's why there's big money in it."

"Why is the risk so high?"

"We're going after a man."

"One man?" Borders asked. "How high can that risk be?"

"But who's the man?" Barnes asked.

Dillon looked at all three of them in turn, then centered on Barnes and said, "Clint Adams."

"Adams," Walden said. "That name sounds—"

"The Gunsmith?" Sam Barnes said. "We gotta go after the Gunsmith?"

"I knew that name sounded—"

"He's still only one man," Jack Borders said.

"Yeah, but the Gunsmith," Barnes said, shaking his head, "I don't know."

"Look," Dillon said, "I'm gonna take him myself. I just need the three of you for backup."

"You? Against the Gunsmith?" Mike Walden asked. "I gotta see that."

"I'd pay to see that," Borders said.

"You think you can take him, Dillon?" Barnes asked.

"Would I take the job if I didn't?"

"What the heck is the Gunsmith doin' in Alton?" Mike Walden asked.

"And who did he get mad at him?" Borders asked.

"None of that matters," Dillon said. "All that matters is that we're being paid a lot of money to get him out of Alton."

"Not to kill him?" Barnes asked.

"To get him out of Alton," Dillon said again, "any way I see fit."

Walden nodded and said, "By killin' him."

Dillon had formed a plan overnight, and he outlined it to the three men.

"Do you think that's gonna work?" Barnes asked.

"You ever seen Melissa Lawrence?" Dillon asked.

"I have," Walden said. "I'd give a month's pay—"

"Yeah, well, Dillon gets her for nothin', don't ya, Dillon?" Borders said.

"That's right," Dillon said. "I keep her happy, and she'll do whatever I want her to."

"So it's a good plan," Walden said.

"It's a great plan," Dillon said, "and it'll work. We all just have to do our part."

"We'll do our part," Walden said.

"You bet," Barnes said.

But leave it to Jack Borders to ask, "When do we get paid?"

FORTY-ONE

The next morning Clint was having breakfast in the hotel dining room, keeping one eye on the door. He knew he wasn't going to get through this meal without somebody interrupting him. He just hoped it was one or both of the detectives, Garrett and Stevens.

As if he'd made a wish and blown out the candles on a cake, both men walked in as he was finishing up.

"Another pot of coffee and two cups," he told the waiter.

"Yes, sir, and will the gentlemen be eating?"

"I hope not," Clint said. "I don't know if I'd be able to afford it."

"Yes, sir."

The two detectives approached the table, both looking grim.

"You haven't come to arrest me, have you?" Clint asked.

"We're making an arrest today," Garrett said, "but it's not you. Mind if we sit?"

"Go ahead."

Both men took a seat, and the waiter came over with the coffee and filled the extra two cups.

"Will that be all?" he asked.

"That's fine," Garrett said, "we don't have an appetite this morning."

"Tell me about it," Clint said when the waiter walked away.

"We got back from Elsah early this morning," Garrett said, "with the name of our killer."

"Which is?"

"Edward Lawrence."

Clint whistled soundlessly and sat back in his chair.

"No wonder you don't have an appetite."

"Yeah," Garrett said, and Stevens just scowled.

"You have to arrest the son of the richest man in Alton?"

"Don't rub it in," Garrett said, sipping his coffee.

"How'd you find out?"

"We got a witness who saw him with the girl," Garrett said, "last one to be with her."

"That's all? Nobody saw him do it?"

"Same witness saw him leave her crib. She was found ten minutes later. Can't be much doubt."

Clint thought about the smiling young man he'd met on the steps of the library, who wanted to take his sister to lunch.

"How are you going to go about it?"

"Try to find him at the father's house, I guess," Garrett said. "We don't know if he lives there or not, but it's a start."

"How do your superiors feel about this?"

"They're scrambling around, looking for holes to hide in," Garrett said. "Can't say I blame them."

"Cowards," Stevens said with a sneer.

"What about letting the boy get away with it?" Clint asked.

Garrett stared at him and said, "Not an option for us.

We'll arrest him. If they want to let him go they'll have to do it themselves.''

Garrett stood up and Stevens followed.

"You're free to go, by the way," Garrett said. "Hope you enjoyed your stay in our city.''

"I've had better times," Clint said, "but then I've had worse.''

As they started to walk away, Stevens turned back and asked, "Did you find anything more on the Piasa bird painting?''

"No," Clint said, "nothing. I guess I'll just have to be satisfied with knowing when it was found, not who painted it.''

Stevens looked as if he was going to leave but stopped again.

"It's been seen.''

"What?''

"There have been sightings, near the bluff, on the bluff,'' the man continued. "People have claimed to have seen the Piasa bird.''

Clint thought about the feather that was still in his saddlebags. Did he dare tell Stevens?

"Have you ever seen it?'' he asked instead.

"No," the detective said, "but you have . . . haven't you?''

He turned and left without giving Clint a chance to reply.

FORTY-TWO

Melissa Lawrence knew she was taking a big chance, but she didn't feel she had a choice.

She entered the hotel only moments after the detectives had left. She hadn't seen them and, in fact, wouldn't have known them if she had.

She went to the front desk. The clerk looked up, saw her, and his jaw dropped. Even though he was the one she had paid to let her into Clint's room, he was still stunned by her beauty.

"Uh—uh—"

"Mr. Clint Adams, please?"

"I—I—think he's still—uh, he's in the dining room, having breakfast."

"Thank you."

She walked to the entrance of the dining room and stopped there, drawing the attention of every man in the room—including Clint. He waved to her and she started for his table.

"What brings you here?" he asked. He didn't know yet if he was going to tell her about her brother.

"I have something to tell you," she said, sitting across from him. "Something real important . . ."

• • •

"You really think he'll come?" Walden asked Dillon.

"He'll come."

"If Melissa Lawrence is persuasive enough," Barnes said.

"She will be."

They were in a clearing just outside the city limits. There was enough cover around it to hide Walden, Barnes, and Borders. Dillon intended to be standing right in the center when Clint Adams arrived.

"Do you all understand now?" Dillon asked.

"Yep," Borders said, "the minute you look like you're in trouble we take him."

"Anybody have a problem with shooting him from here?" Dillon asked.

"You kiddin'?" Barnes asked. "I prefer doin' it from here than facin' him. I don't envy you, Dillon."

"I hope you can take him," Walden said.

"I hope so, too," Dillon said.

"Wouldn't you rather do this where there are witnesses?" Borders asked.

"You three will be my witnesses," Dillon said. "When I ride back into town with the Gunsmith slung over his saddle, it won't matter. Everyone will believe I killed him, and you three will back me up."

"Oh, we'll back you up, all right," Walden said. "We're gettin' paid enough."

"It's almost time," Dillon said. "I'm gonna get in the clearing. Everybody just remember the signal."

"Yeah," Walden said, "if he kills you, we kill him."

Dillon gave the man a dirty look.

"Okay, okay," Walden said, "we'll watch you. If you take your hat off that's our signal to take him. It means you've decided not to do it yourself."

"Not to take the risk," Borders said.

"I think that's the way we should do it, anyway," Barnes said.

"I'm touched by your concern, Sam."

"Concern, hell," Barnes said, "if you get killed we don't get paid, because we don't know who we're doin' this job for."

"You fellas are working for me," Dillon said. "And don't worry, you'll get paid."

Dillon left them to spread out and hide themselves while he stood right in the center of the clearing.

FORTY-THREE

Clint found the clearing with no problem, right where Melissa said it would be. He could see the man standing in the center of it, and assumed that this was the man she called Dillon. He stopped far enough away to keep Duke out of the line of fire and dismounted. He dropped the big gelding's reins to the ground and walked to the clearing.

"That's far enough," Dillon said as Clint entered the clearing.

"You Dillon?"

"That's right," Dillon said. "And you're Adams?"

"I am."

"You came alone?"

"That's what I was told," Clint said. "You're supposed to have some information for me?"

"That's right," Dillon said. "I'm supposed to, but I don't."

Clint frowned. "I don't understand. What are you talking about?"

"I'm not here to give you information on some stupid bird, Adams," Dillon said. "I'm here to kill you."

"Oh, I see," Clint said. He looked around, but didn't see anyone. "You came alone?"

"Think I can't take you alone?" Dillon asked.

"I think you're too smart to try, Dillon."

"What?"

"Sure, a smart guy like you, smart enough to lure me out here, you're also too smart to take a chance on getting killed. Why take a chance that maybe I'm as fast as my reputation?"

"I'm fast, Adams," Dillon said. "Damn fast."

"I don't doubt that you are, Dillon," Clint said. "But I'll let you in on a little secret."

"What's that?"

"Of all the men I've killed in a fair fight," Clint lied, "some of them were faster than I was."

"What?"

"That's right," Clint said, "but none of them shot straighter. See, it doesn't matter how fast you can get your gun out if you can't shoot straight."

"I can shoot straight enough," Dillon said, but his hands were sweating. There was too much talking already. What if Adams was right? What if he outdrew the Gunsmith but his shot missed? He wouldn't get another one.

"You'll only have one chance at this, Dillon," Clint said. "You'd better make the most of it."

Dillon's palms were slick now. He was starting to think that his gun might even slip out of his hand when he drew it.

"Come on, Dillon," Clint said. "We might as well get this over with."

"It's hot," Dillon said and reached for his hat with his left hand. He took it off, held it for a moment, then wiped his forehead with his sleeve and replaced the hat.

What happened? There should have been shots by now.

"Better try it again," Clint said.

"Try what again?" Dillon asked.

"The hat," Clint said. "That's the signal, isn't it? For

your men to gun me down? Taking off your hat? Try it again.''

Dillon snatched his hat from his head with his left hand and waved it this time, but nothing happened.

''Come on!'' he shouted. ''What are you waitin' for?''

''They can't shoot, Dillon,'' Clint said. ''They don't have their guns.''

''W-what?''

''I met some friendly fellas in a tavern the other day, and when Melissa told me you were setting a trap for me I went and found them down by the docks.''

''She told you?''

''What did you think, she'd really send me into your trap to be killed? You've got an exaggerated idea of how much she likes being with you.''

''I don't—what's goin' on?''

''My friends have disarmed your friends by now,'' Clint said. ''If they hadn't I'd be dead by now, so we can safely assume that it's now just you and me.''

Dillon wet his lips and put his hat back on.

''I don't need no help.''

''Fine,'' Clint said, ''then dry your hands on your thighs and do what you've got to do.''

Dillon flexed his hands, the palms of which were now slick and sticky. He did as Clint said, wiped his hands on his thighs, but as he brought his right hand up he went right for his gun, hoping to surprise Clint.

Clint was watching the man closely. He really didn't think Dillon had it in him to go for his gun, but damned if he didn't try to do it sneaky-like, while drying his hands.

Clint drew his gun and fired once. Dillon's gun never cleared leather, and he fell facedown in the center of the clearing, dead.

Clint holstered his gun and walked to the body to make sure he was dead. When he was sure he looked up and saw Dillon's three friends being marched out of the brush by six of the men Clint had been buying drinks for that first night.

"Any of you men want your guns back?" he asked.

The three men exchanged glances, and one of them—Walden—said, "No, sir."

"Okay," Clint said to his friends, "let them go."

"You sure?"

He nodded, and the three men were released.

The two men who had flanked him at the bar that night came and stood on either side of him again.

"If you'd told us who you was that first night," one of them said, "we woulda bought you drinks."

"Didn't I tell you?"

"No," the other man said.

"I don't remember," Clint said. "What the heck did you fellas have me drinking that night, anyway?"

"Rum," the first man said. "A seaman's drink."

"Dark rum," the second man said. "And lots of it."

"Sometimes," the first man said, "it clouds a man's thinkin'."

Clint put a hand on each of their shoulders and said, "Now you tell me."

EPILOGUE

It was pure luck, of course. Luck that Clint had found the bartender in the tavern that early, and luck that the man had been able to direct him to where to find the men he needed.

As they got back to the city Clint promised to meet the men again that night for a farewell drink, as he told them he was leaving the next day.

"We'll be a-waitin'," the men told him.

"And no rum this time," Clint said. "Just beer for me."

One of the men cackled and said, "We'll see."

When Clint got back to the hotel, Melissa was waiting in the lobby.

"Well?" she asked.

"Dillon's dead," Clint said.

"What about the others?"

"I let them go."

"But—"

"They won't come around," Clint said. "They were being paid by Dillon, and now he's dead. There's no one to pay them. Melissa, I want to thank you again for warning me."

"I didn't have a choice," she said. "I couldn't send you to be killed."

He was about to answer when suddenly Emma Lawrence came running into the lobby.

"Emma!"

"Melissa," she said. "What are you doing here?"

"I was warning Clint about Dillon . . . but he's dead now. Clint killed him. What's wrong?"

"Melissa," Emma said, "the police have arrested Eddie."

"What for?"

"They say he's the one who killed that girl in Elsah," Emma said, looking at Clint. "Clint . . . I didn't know what to do."

"There's only one thing to do, Emma," Clint said, including Melissa in the statement. "You have to go and be with your family."

"But . . . I don't know if he did it," Emma said.

"He's still your brother," Clint said. "Go and be with him and your family. Does your father know?"

She nodded. "He's getting a lawyer."

"Then go, both of you."

Emma looked at Melissa, who said, "Wait outside, Em. I'll be right there."

Emma nodded and went outside.

"What is it, Melissa?" Clint asked.

"Was the dead girl named Ellie?" she asked.

"Yes, she was. Why?"

"Eddie talked about her," Melissa said. "He told me about her. Clint . . . I—I think he did it."

Clint hesitated a moment, then said, "Well, since I knew the lady slightly I'd be inclined to say she somehow drove him to it."

"You're leaving, aren't you?" she asked.

"Tomorrow."

"This thing with Eddie . . . we won't have time . . ." she said.

"Say good-bye now, Melissa," he said, "and then go and be with your family."

She gave him a hug and said, "I have a feeling if we'd had half a chance, you would have been the best man I ever knew."

"I think," he said, releasing her from his arms, "that you still have plenty of time to meet the best man you're ever going to know, Melissa."

She squeezed his hand once and then went out to join her sister.

That night Clint went back to the no name tavern on Front Street, just off of Broadway, and drank with the men there until early in the morning. One by one the men bid him farewell and left, until he was left with the original two men who had braced him at the bar that night. He didn't remember their names, and didn't want to admit it. What did it matter? He probably wouldn't be back here again, anyway.

"What was it you came here for in the first place, mate?" the first man asked.

Clint had stuck to beer, but the other two men had been drinking rum, so they were very drunk.

"The Piasa bird," Clint said. "I was trying to find out about the Piasa bird."

"I know that bird," the second man said. "The one on the bluff, right? The painting?"

"That's right," Clint said. "What do you know about it?"

"I know old Charlie, the Illini Indian, hangs around up there."

"I was told about him," Clint said, "but I never found him."

"Maybe you saw him up there," the man said.

"No, I only saw . . ."

"Saw what?"

"Never mind."

The second man looked at the first one.

"He saw it," he said.

The first man laughed.

"Saw what?" Clint asked.

"You saw the bird," the second man said, and they both laughed.

Clint thought the two men were too drunk to know what they were talking about.

"There's no such bird," he said.

"There is," the first man said.

Then the second one added, "When old Charlie dresses up."

"What?"

"Charlie," the second man said through his laughter, "gets himself all got up in feathers to try and scare people."

"How do you know that?"

"Hell, we've drunk with the old Indian," the first man said.

"Holds his rum better than you'd think, for an Indian," the second one said. "You want to talk to him?"

"Can you arrange it?" Clint asked.

"Hell," the man said, "all you got to do is go up on that bluff and sit there with a bottle of rum. He'll find you."

"You shoulda told us this the first night," the first man said. "We coulda saved ya a lot of trouble."

"Yep," Clint said, "you sure could have."

Clint left the no-name tavern and his no-name friends, taking a bottle of rum with him. The next morning he rode back to the bluff—past Elsah, without stopping in—and made his way to the top again. He found himself a rock, set the bottle of rum down on the ground between his legs, and settled down to wait.

Watch for

KANSAS CITY KILLING

207th novel in the exciting GUNSMITH series
from Jove

Coming in April!

J. R. ROBERTS
THE
GUNSMITH